LAST OF THE GARGOYLES BOOK 3

THE REDEEMED

FoxTales Press

DANI HOOTS

The Redeemed
Last of the Gargoyles, #3
© 2021 Dani Hoots
Cover Design Copyright © 2021 by Biserka Designs
Formatting by Dani Hoots
All rights reserved.

ISBN for paperback: 978-1-942023-85-2

ISBN for hardcover: 978-1-942023-86-9

CHAPTER ONE

Gwen took a slow breath in and out, watching a little cloud appear in front of her face.

It was chilly Christmas Day in Tokyo. Couples and friends were out partying and having a good time. Gwen always loved spending Christmas in Japan as most didn't consider it a religious holiday but one for lovers to enjoy. It was like Valentine's Day but with gifts and pretty lights, and snow if she were farther into the mountains.

She held on to James's arm and set her head onto his shoulder. "It's romantic, don't you think?"

James glanced at her. "You do realize this day

celebrates everything we conspire against, right?"

"I do, but that's not how it is viewed here. In Japan it's just some romantic holiday."

"Fair enough. The lights do make it pretty. It's sure cold though."

"It's warmer than Russia," Gwen teased.

"Most places are warmer than Russia." He placed his hand on her arm, which was linked in his other arm. "Now, what all do you want to see tonight?"

Gwen smiled ear to ear. "I heard Meguro River has a really pretty light show."

"Well then," James said. "Lead the way."

It amazed Gwen all the places one could travel within Tokyo with their rail systems. Although they were packed more often than not, they still were more advanced than anything in Europe. They got onto the Toei Asakusa line and headed toward the closest station for the Meguro River Minna-no-Illumination, which by the map seemed to be Gotanda Station.

Gwen held on to James as he was able to grab a handle. They both had pretty good balance, but being around all these people always made them anxious. Gwen could sense the blood they all possessed and did her best not to give in to her hunger. It had been a couple of days since she'd truly fed as they had been busy creating minions, and that never quite hit the spot.

James kissed the top of her head.

She peered up at him. "What was that for?"

"Can't I kiss you?"

She grinned and leaned in to kiss him on the lips. She could feel the stares and the cold shoulder that the other passengers were giving them, but she didn't care. She was with the man she loved and had always loved for centuries.

They reached their destination and hopped off the train a little forcibly as it was over capacity. They made their way out of the station and took a deep breath of the cold air. Hundreds of people still crowded them as they headed toward the light show, but she felt a bit more free now that she was off the train.

"Are you sure you want to go somewhere crowded? We could just go back to the hotel and have a little alone time." James brushed his finger on her cheek.

She rolled her eyes. "We always have alone time. Come on. I want to see the beauty of this place before the entire world is overrun by demons."

He sighed. "Fine. If you say so."

Gwen skipped as they snaked their way through the

crowd. She gasped as her eyes took in the beauty of the lights. Normally during the spring the area was covered in sakura blossoms as far as the eye could see. For the winter, however, the trees were wrapped in pink lights to mimic the fantastic sight.

She glanced over to James, who was captured in awe as much as she was. He saw her staring at him, and his face softened. "Fine, you are right. These are beautiful."

Gwen beamed at him as they slowly made their way forward with the crowd of people who were also taking in the sights. Japan knew how to put on a show using nature, and she respected that. The world was beautiful, and she didn't want it to change even though she had witnessed so much change over the centuries. If she could, she would go back to when humans hadn't altered so much of it. But one couldn't change the past —she knew that painfully more than most.

As they made their way through the riverside, Gwen couldn't help but lose herself in her thoughts. So much had happened in the past few months that she wasn't sure what would happen next. They had taken down two Gargoyles, and now there was only one left—one before they could open the gates of hell. Would they succeed? Would they be able to get their revenge on

Heaven and bring hell to Earth? Would it be everything they had dreamed? Or would it be a bunch of lies, just as it always was?

Then there was the issue of Collin. Gwen knew she should have killed him when she had the chance with Elizabeth, but something made her want to let him live. Did she still care for him? Perhaps. Or perhaps, deep down, she wanted someone to be able to stop her in the end.

She glanced to James, whose attention was still on the lights. He was the best at reading her mind and her guilt. He couldn't know she was still having second thoughts even after everything she had done in the past few months. He loved her more than anything in the world, and the more she doubted herself and what they were doing, the more she feared he would walk away from her.

She knew that James's love for her was never changing, but after she'd left him in Germany all those decades ago, she had broken his trust. She didn't want to see that look on his face again, so she decided she would keep her doubts bottled inside. But keeping it bottled inside meant it would explode and her subconscious would do stupid things.

Like let Collin get away.

James turned to her and brushed a piece of her red hair out of her face. Her hair was getting longer now, and instead of being in a bob, it was down to her collarbones. "What is wrong, my love?"

"Nothing," Gwen said as she squeezed his arm. "I just lost myself in the beauty of this place."

He didn't comment. He knew that was a lie. There was always something on her mind. They had been together for such a long time that they understood each other in and out. So she could tell he was watching her, feeling her out to see what she would do next.

She couldn't do anything to jeopardize this—otherwise she would be tortured for all eternity. Literally.

Lucifer had a special place waiting for her if she screwed this up. He'd made that very clear when he stepped on Earth a little over a month ago. She also knew that he had a special place for James, and that scared her even more. He didn't deserve the punishment—she did. James did everything in his power to serve Lucifer—all of them had. And yet if things didn't go the way Lucifer wanted, then they were blamed.

It was why she was having second thoughts. She had seen his lies again and again and had begun to realize perhaps he wasn't the best leader—and perhaps all his promises were lies. But she had to tell herself it wasn't as if Heaven was much better as she could love who she wanted to love.

All this had been for James, and she would never lose that love for him.

Granted, that meant everything around her would be destroyed. She figured that the paradise Lucifer so viciously wanted wouldn't leave much in the way of beauty as he hated anything that he thought might surpass him. It was quite sad, to be honest.

The trees, now slumbering for the winter, would appear in the spring as magnificent pink giants that thousands upon thousands would travel to come see. Gwen honestly didn't think anything in this world was more beautiful, which meant that they would probably be the first to go in Lucifer's new world order. That, or he would make them part of his personal kingdom. It could go either way. Gwen wondered if she could sneak some mirrors into his room and distract him for a century or two. It was possible as it had happened before.

She shook her head a little, wanting to draw herself out of her own thoughts. She needed to focus on the now—she needed to focus on James and how handsome he appeared in his double-breasted black coat, dark green turtleneck, and dark jeans. Well, she didn't care for the turtleneck as she did like seeing the skin on his neck where she loved to bite him. She wanted more than anything to nibble on his skin right then and there, but that would draw more attention than they wanted at that moment.

It was just the two of them in Japan, turning the right people needed to cause chaos at a moment's notice. The others were taking over different countries in Asia. As for Erik and Collin, she hadn't heard a peep out of either of them. It was more than likely they were hiding in the Vatican as it was close to off-limits for them, at least until they gathered a big enough army to destroy it. Then Erik would have to fight.

But that was in the future, and she had to focus on the present. They would leave the following morning for Hong Kong—another place she hadn't visited in quite some time. There they would discuss their plan of action, and it would just be work from there on out until the gate was opened.

So it was moments like these she tried to cherish—moments where she almost felt human and could love the man she wanted without consequence. She peered up at the pink lights, wishing that this second would last until the end of time—knowing it could be the last incident she was happy.

"Why don't we go find something to eat?" James asked, bringing her out of her delusion of being anything remotely human.

She flashed a fang at him. "Lead the way."

CHAPTER TWO

Collin paced back and forth on the balcony, watching the crowd below try to gather below. They wanted to be as close as they could to the pope while he gave Christmas Eve mass. Although he was fighting for God, he didn't care to go down to listen to a man speak ofAngels and God when he himself was the only one who was fighting in a holy war.

Collin wondered if the Crusaders had included the Gargoyles and demons and decided that was a stupid question. Anything noteworthy in history seemed to have to do with these creatures of a different realm. Humans were just collateral. It was strange to think we were so important in the eyes of the Lord when he also had created beings like Erik and Elizabeth.

Elizabeth.

He still couldn't believe she was gone. Gwen had tortured her, made her cry, pleading for her life. And she had done it all in front of Collin, letting him realize it was because of his trust in Gwen that she was able to kill Elizabeth. He would never trust her again.

The problem was now he thirsted for blood even more. He hadn't had Gwen's blood in quite some time, and it felt as if he was going to go feral. Collin couldn't bring himself to drink human blood, but he wasn't sure he was going to have much of a choice here soon.

He could go after humans who were what society deemed bad—ones who hurt others even though there was another way out. But even then he wasn't sure he could do it—he didn't know if he could put a human life in his hand.

Because right now it was the only thing that made him feel he was different from a demon.

If he killed a human, innocent or not, he was no different than them. Could he really face that realization? Would he still go to Heaven, or would he be tortured in hell for an eternity with the Twelve

Generals of Lucifer? Even though Erik had assured him that he would go to Heaven, Collin couldn't help but wonder.

The figure in the distance, whom most people wouldn't be able to identify but with his demon-like eyes he could distinguish as the pope, began to pray. Collin felt strange being in this city as he didn't see himself as anything good. He fed off blood—he had been in a relationship with a demon. If that didn't mean he was damned, he wasn't sure what did.

He also watched as the people who crowded the streets began to pray. Collin wondered what they prayed for—if it was personal, for someone else, or if they were praying that the world wouldn't be overrun by demons who were trying to open the gates of hell. It probably wasn't that last one as none of them knew the true terrors that were about to come.

Collin was having his doubts about, well, everything. The demons were strong, and only Erik was left. Collin didn't believe himself an asset as he had caused the death of Elizabeth. What if he messed up again? What if Erik died? Would it be up to Collin to stop the demons? Would it even matter, or would the gates automatically open the moment Erik died and Collin would just have to witness the destruction of the Earth? Knowing the demons, they would probably keep him alive and tied up somewhere, eyes taped open so he could watch forever.

It would be his own personal hell.

Deciding he needed to step away from these darker thoughts which seemed to cloud his mind more often than not, he stepped inside, where Erik was making a mocha. Neither of them needed caffeine as both their energies required other means, but Collin had to admit having coffee made from a moka pot was delicious. He had never had coffee taste so good before. It was served in small cups, similar to espresso but not as strong. It seemed as if that was all they drank in Italy, and they did so religiously.

"Here you go," Erik said as he placed the cup on the table where Collin had taken a seat. Steam lifted off the dark liquid and smelled of rich chocolate and hazelnuts.

"Thank you." He held the warm cup in his hands. It had been cold outside, and although it felt good to calm down, now he wanted to warm up.

"It is pretty crowded out there, isn't it?" Erik blew on his own cup.

"That it is. And yet none of them know the truth."

"That a creature of Heaven is just on the other side of town?" Erik chuckled. "It always made Hugo want to go out there and fly around. We stopped him, of course."

Collin laughed a little. "I could see him doing that. He seemed like someone who liked to play tricks and have a good laugh."

"That he did. He's probably laughing it up in Heaven as we speak."

They were silent for a moment as Collin realized that Erik was alone now. He didn't have any of his kind he could talk to. Granted, when he died, he would get to see them. But with his death, it would either mean victory or defeat. Everything was riding on him and him alone. Collin realized some of it was on him as well, but it didn't feel that way—it felt as if he were in the way.

"Elizabeth's plan should have worked. We should have been able to kill all four of them."

Erik smiled, but it was an empty smile. "You are right, but they got lucky as they always do. But we shouldn't think about the past—we should plan for the future."

"Which is what? We have been hiding here for over a

month now. You have seen the news. It appears that they went to Asia and have been mucking around there. It is only a matter of time before they come back for us. For you."

"Indeed, and it will be the last fight to determine the future of Earth."

Collin shook his head. "But why can't you just keep hiding? Why can't you just stay in the church? They can't come into Vatican City, can they? I mean, I suppose they could, but it would be like them going into a church—a lot of risk."

Erik sipped his mocha. "Well, they can't come into Vatican City because it is surrounded by a barrier of salt underneath the entire area. But while we are outside it in Rome, they can sense us. But out here, you can sense them easier too."

I hadn't known that. It made sense, though, as I couldn't sense Erik when they stepped inside the city limits. I had assumed it was because of all the churches and such.

"Ah. So why don't we stay here until the end of time?"

"Because they will burn the entire world down to get me. For now we just need to prepare and think of a way to take them down. They aren't attacking, which is good. But who knows how long that will last? Right now it is time to rest and evaluate where we are."

Where they were was trapped with demons rampaging through the lands, Collin thought. He sighed as he knew there was no point in saying it out loud. Erik was wiser than him, and he wasn't going to understand what the point of waiting was. He just wanted it all to be over—he wanted to be done.

He just wanted this thirst to be over with.

Erik took a sip of his mocha again. "You're hungry, aren't you?"

Collin held back a sarcastic retort. "Yeah. It's increasing by the day. I'm not sure how much longer I can hold on."

"We can try my blood again, although it didn't work in Berlin. It doesn't hurt to try—it seems you changed after Moscow."

Collin knew he had changed since then but didn't want to admit it. After what Gwen had done to him, he felt as if he had had his heart ripped out of his chest by the woman he had once loved. If he didn't know better, he would think his heart was missing and he was a walking husk hell-bent on revenge—and saving the world of course.

"Yeah, sure."

Erik stood up, as did Collin. He never knew how to go about this. With Gwen, it was intimate as he wanted her skin close to his, but with anyone else, it was a whole matter of who stood where, or should he sit? Erik handed him his wrist, and Collin bit down.

Blood came pouring into his mouth, and for the first time, it tasted like sweet wine and honey. When he drank the Gargoyles' blood before, it still had the foul stench that it had when he was human. Did this mean he was growing more comfortable with his new nature? Or did it mean, now that his heart was broken and he didn't seek out Gwen, he could focus on fulfilling his bloodlust another way? He wasn't sure, and he didn't know if he wanted to find out the answer.

He knew he should stop drinking the blood, but it had been so long since he had his fill. It felt wondrous, like pure energy. It reminded him of Gwen, and at that moment he let go. He didn't want to be like her—he didn't want to see the blood that stained her hands.

Collin wanted more than anything to forget her.

"Did that help?" Erik asked as he went into the kitchen and grabbed a cloth to wipe the blood away. He threw one to Collin.

Collin nodded. "Yeah. It surprisingly did."

"Well, that's good. Do you have an idea why it would have changed like that?"

He hesitated, not sure if he should tell Erik how he was feeling about everything, mainly Gwen. So far they hadn't brought her up, and he had a feeling it was mainly so Collin was given time to process what had happened. He shook his head. "Honestly, I don't. Perhaps my body finally decided not to be dependent on one source of blood."

Erik examined him for a moment, as if he was debating what to say. "Yeah, perhaps it did. Lucky for us."

"Yeah," Collin repeated. "Lucky."

CHAPTER THREE

James could tell by the way Gwen was losing herself in her head that she was up to something. Or perhaps she wasn't and she truly had a lot on her mind, but it was more than likely not the case. She was having regrets. Again.

He squeezed her hand, which was wrapped around his arm. He loved her more than anything. He would fall from Heaven all over again for her, and he knew she would do the same. So why was she second-guessing now? Did she really want to spend all eternity being tortured together? Earth had much better accommodations. She was a fool to think Lucifer was lying about what hell would be like for us—what hell was like for those who had already fallen.

Or perhaps she wasn't thinking about betraying them again. Perhaps she was thinking about how she wanted to see these trees when they were truly blooming instead of lights making it appear like they were blooming. He had to admit they were a sight to see, and he hoped that Lucifer and his army wouldn't destroy them. This world was beautiful, and it would be more beautiful once they were in charge.

Things just had to go smoothly from here on out. And how would they not? There was only one Gargoyles left and four of them. Even with that hybrid, there was no way they could win. Collin was too weak—too weak with Gwen being able to trick him the way she did.

James realized that was more than likely the reason Gwen was acting the way that she was. She still had feelings for the boy, and no matter how many times she swore that he meant nothing to her, James could tell she was lying. It didn't bother him that she fell for a human that made her feel human herself. No, what bothered him was the fact that she kept lying about it. He needed the truth from her, and yet she never gave it to him.

"So, where should we look for a bite to eat?" Gwen

turned to him, her eyes flashing yellow.

He patted her hand. "Don't worry, my love. I know just the place."

And he did. They made their way to a station to the north of the lights and shuffled into a train. Although James liked how easy it was to get around in Japan, he did not like traveling during busy times like holidays. But it was a minor inconvenience, and his irritation would be rewarded as they made their way to Ikebukuro.

It was a long trip, about forty minutes, but it was an area he was familiar with. Before he went to America to work, he had spent some time in Japan looking for Gwen, only to come up short. He had really thought she would hide here, especially since she loved it so much. Alas, she had been hiding out in Europe, following Erik.

"So, where are we going?" Gwen asked. "I presume somewhere this line takes us?"

He nodded. "You assume correctly. We are going to Ikebukuro."

"Ooh, I do love that area. There's always something going on there."

"And there is a yakuza headquarters there. Figured

we could find some strays to drain."

She hugged him and kissed him on the lips. "You always think of everything."

"That I do." He kissed her again, even though he knew people around him were staring. He didn't care—soon they would rule this entire world.

As long as everything went according to plan, he told himself. Except nothing ever did, hence they were still trying to open the gates two thousand years later.

Originally the mission had been to take down the Son of God. And they did—they got everyone to betray him. They even killed him, and yet that didn't work. Lucifer had lied, and the Son rose again, causing even more people to have faith in him.

But this time had to be different, didn't it? They couldn't lose again. The end was coming. They would finally get their chance to rule.

"You know," Gwen began, "it's so silly that they pick this night for the Son of God to be born. I mean, it used to be our holiday. We used to ride around, destroying anyone who was out on those cold, dark nights. And yet the Christians stole it from us."

James smiled at the memory. "Those were the days. It was so cold back then in the north. But it was a lot of fun."

"That it was. Perhaps the Gargoyles were the reason the church decided to make it that day. They wanted to throw us off."

"As if they could ever throw us off," James added.

Gwen swayed back and forth, biting her lip. "They have a few times. But it is rare. Most of the ones that really threw us for a loop are gone now." She grinned. "Like Elizabeth."

"You really hated her, didn't you?"

She nodded. "That I did. She was smart and strategized in a way that made it so I never could have any fun. She has killed quite a few of us. And then Darrell. I was glad I could watch her suffer at the end. It was all the more satisfying."

James had seen the look in Gwen's eyes when she killed Elizabeth. It had been one of pure bliss. He was glad that she was at least that much back to normal, but perhaps it was more for revenge that she was able to give the final blow.

He traced his finger on his cheek. "But you hesitated killing Collin and let him escape, knowing full well Erik would come back for him."

Gwen narrowed her eyes at him. "What are you

trying to say?"

James shrugged. "That you aren't quite truthful about what you want. It is as if you don't know yourself."

Gwen stared up at him as if trying to read him. He didn't look away but kept a steady gaze on her. Her eyes flickered, and she leaned her head on her chest.

"I'm not sure, James. I want to be with you forever, but there's just always something there, like a voice in the back of my head. I don't want it to be there, I swear. But it is, and it won't shut up."

He wrapped his arms around her. "Well, at least you are being honest with me."

She didn't say anything, and they stayed silent for the rest of the ride over to Ikebukuro. They got off the train and made their way into the district.

"Are we just looking for some people who are alone?" Gwen asked as they headed toward the back alleyways and away from the major streets.

James nodded. "Of course, unless you want to start a panic."

She smiled. "I don't mind, but I think Jamesie would get in a big drama fit."

James chuckled. That was true. He did like to make a mountain out of a molehill. But after everything that happened, he and Gwen knew that they needed to be on the down low.

They made their way through the maze of streets and came across an area that was deserted other than a couple of humans who were smoking. Although they were covered with coats, James could see the tattoos that covered their hands as they pulled their cigarettes from their mouths.

"Looks like we got some contenders," Gwen whispered as her eyes turned yellow.

With a flash, she ran over and bit into the neck of the man on the right. Before the second man could scream, James rushed over and bit into his neck.

It had been a while since they had actually fed on humans versus turning minions. They had been busy working and had simply been feeding off each other. Although it was more pleasant than drinking from a human, as they were more intimate, it didn't quite hit the spot in the end. It gave them more power, of course, but they had to have their human meter filled up as well, so to speak.

Gwen let the body collapse at her feet as she wiped the blood away from her face. "Ahhh. That hit the spot."

James licked his lips as he dropped his person. "Should we look for more humans, my love?"

She shook her head as she stepped close to him. "No, I think we should head back and get our fill a different way."

He grinned. "I like the way you think."

CHAPTER FOUR

Erik didn't want to tell Collin the truth.

There was no way they were going to be able to stop the demons. Erik had spent the past month trying to come up with some plan—some way to defeat the demons—but he couldn't come up with anything. He communed with Michael and Gabriel and other Archangels, but none of them would give him a clear answer. They said help would be unfair even though the demons got help from Lucifer time after time. Evil never played fair, he knew.

Erik wouldn't give up, however, and would die fighting. But he would be the one bringing the fate of good versus evil to Heaven, and that was what made him feel all the worse about it. All the others who had passed laid their hope on him, and he knew it was misguided faith. He wasn't smart, and he had stained his hands in the blood that was Guinevere just so he could have one more ally. But that didn't help the odds; he knew that now. In fact, it might have made them even worse.

He didn't blame Collin for what had happened, far from it. He truly believed in Gwen, and Erik had thought he and his comrades had performed all the major steps to make sure she didn't betray them. Collin could sense the others across the city. There was no way they would have realized the demons were covered in Gwen's blood and assumingly had buckets of blood across town so that Collin would sense something.

It was beyond disgusting and dark. Erik had seen his fair share of gore, especially when dealing with Gwen, but it was something completely different to see a person completely crusted in blood moving around as if it were nothing. Only a demon would ever do, or think, of such a tactic.

So now they couldn't even trust Collin's senses as to where the demons were. He doubted they would try that

tactic again as now they only needed to take him out—
Gwen wouldn't trust Collin with anything or be able to
use him again. Any feelings for Gwen were completely
gone—that much was apparent in Collin's eyes. He
appeared to be someone who had lost hope in love, and
Erik felt pity for him.

But that was what happened when you fell in love
with a demon—pain and disappointment.

It was a pain Erik was glad he didn't have to feel as
Heavenly beings didn't love one another like humans
did. That was why some of theAngels fell and became
demons—because they wanted to feel such things. But
the love that they felt was selfish and wrong. Their love
came at the price of evil and darkness, condemning
themselves to hell, whereas human love was a lot more
pure than that. Human love was about being together as
one and selflessness. Or at least that was how Erik saw
it. Perhaps he was wrong as he'd seen a lot of horrible
things come out of human love throughout history.
Perhaps they were all fooling themselves about how
innocent humans were so that they didn't feel as if they
were fighting for nothing.

No, Erik wasn't fighting for humans themselves but
for Heaven and the power of light. He couldn't let

darkness prevail. He couldn't let demons win and destroy everything that their god put into being.

Erik sighed as he collapsed on the couch. Collin was in the shower as he usually was after he fed. It must have been the only way he could cope in dealing with the blood lust. Erik couldn't blame him. The need for blood was like a sin that couldn't be cleansed. But at least for Collin, he was fighting for Heaven and therefore wouldn't be going to hell. Or at least that was what Erik assumed. Collin wasn't dead yet, and he still had a choice. Gwen could somehow tempt him into the darkness that is hell. But he doubted it at this point.

Especially since Collin could finally stomach his blood. Erik wasn't quite sure why that was but figured it had to do with Gwen. The reason he couldn't stomach it earlier must have been mental, which was somewhat good for them. Erik didn't have to worry about Collin snapping, but it also meant he sort of snapped in a sense. He no longer was disgusted by blood and could stomach everyone's and not just Gwen's. But it also meant that Gwen was successful in getting to him in a way.

Collin stepped out of the bathroom fully dressed, but his hair still damp. Erik nodded to him.

"Feel better?"

Collin shrugged. "It only sort of helps. I mean, it won't wash away all the blood that is on my hands. It's been a thing I've been dealing with since Gwen first gave me her blood."

"That's right. You started having nightmares back then, didn't you?"

He nodded. "I never quite understood them. I mean, we killed demons, and so I somewhat felt the truth behind them. But now… seeing what she is willing to do… I get it. They are dreams of the sins of that monster."

That monster. Collin really had lost his faith in her. Erik was glad that this time he wouldn't hesitate to kill her.

Erik stood and peered out the balcony door. People were still around the Vatican, listening to the pope talk. They didn't know that deep down in the catacombs only one candle burned, indicating to the church that only Erik was left to save them all. It wouldn't be like the rapture—all the people believing in God immediately dying like in the stories. No, this was demons coming to Earth and killing them, torturing them, doing whatever the hell they wanted.

Would the humans be able to keep their faith in good if evil reigned? If their life wasn't perfect, or at least somewhat good, would they turn their back on truth? Only time would tell.

Collin stepped up to him. "I remember having to go to mass when I was a kid. It was always so long and so boring."

This made Erik laugh. "That it is. You humans always make a show of everything. Prayer and worship doesn't need to be this big but in everything one does. That got lost somewhere along the way."

"Clearly. It's probably to keep them focused on something. Or to show off. Who knows, really? Each person is different."

Erik smiled as he opened the door. The cool air hit him in an instant as he wasn't wearing a coat. He stepped outside and listened to the Latin being spoken. There was always something beautiful about the language, even though the Latin the church spoke wasn't nearly the same as the ancient language. He didn't understand, however, why people still used it to commune to Heaven. It wasn't like that was what was spoken in Heaven. Or hell, for that matter. God andAngels and demons, all understood each and every language. Otherwise, how would prayers be answered?

But would they be answered? After Erik died, it would be chaos. Would any of their wishes be answered, or would it be complete disorder? It was something Erik felt was all on him. It would be his fault that this world was destroyed—it would be his fault that the humans were all tortured and destroyed.

He let in a slow breath. Why did it have to be him? He wasn't the strongest, the wisest, or the most noble. So why was it him who would have to find a way to destroy four demons?

There was no way—it was impossible.

"You all right?" Collin asked.

Erik peered over at Collin to find him full of concern. Erik gently smiled. "I'm fine. Just a lot to take in."

"But we will win. We have to. Good always prevails, right?"

Erik didn't know if that comment was true or not. Did good always prevail? He had lived through many wars, both on Earth and in Heaven. To him, there never seemed to be a winner. It always seemed like it was a tie, as if there could never be anything but balance.

So what would really happen if he lost? Would something else replace him and stop the demons from winning? And if he won, would more demons be sent into this never-ending struggle? And now that he thought about it, was there really a difference between balance and two people pulling on the ends of a rope?

"Perhaps my defeat is inevitable," he whispered. "Perhaps something was supposed to take my place?"

Collin held up his hands. "Well, don't look at me. I am not up for the task. I can't imagine the stress and burden that are on your shoulders."

Erik chuckled. "Yeah, it's not fun. But I am beginning to wonder what all this is for and whether there will ever really be an end."

"What do you mean?"

He shook his head. "Forget about it. I'm just tired. Tired of all this. I'm ready to go home and see my friends. It's been thousands of years—I'm ready."

Collin studied him for a moment. Erik knew the boy was trying to understand what that felt like, but he had no idea how long that really was. Maybe Collin would one day understand, but he hoped not for the sake of his sanity. He hoped Collin would someday grow old, have a family, and belong. That, however, was more than likely not in the cards for him.

"Just tell me what to do," Collin said.

Erik smiled as he nodded. "All right. Here is what is going to happen."

CHAPTER FIVE

Plane rides were stupid.

Gwen peered down at the ocean below as they flew from Tokyo to Hong Kong. It was a five-hour trip of pure hell. Her tattoo of the chains that bound her to Earth and hell burned her skin. She kept shooting glares at James. He held up his hands in defense.

"Don't look at me. Not my fault this is how everyone gets around now."

She folded her arms in front of herself. "Why didn't the humans focus on high-speed rail on water? Or though the water?"

He kissed her cheek. "How about we plan that for

when we take over the world, hmm? No more planes."

She nodded. "Yes, that will be our first order of business—destroy all planes and make new, better modes of transportation."

James chuckled. "You are so simpleminded. I love that about you."

Gwen raised an eyebrow. "Are you trying to tell me that you don't miss being a pirate at sea, causing chaos wherever we went?"

"I definitely miss that. But you have to admit being able to get places quickly is quite nice. It has made the missions in the past hundred years move along much quicker."

She did have to admit that. Usually it took generations to achieve what they wanted. "But where is the fun in that? We have time."

"Do we though?"

Glancing at him, she wasn't sure what he was getting at. "I mean, we are eternal beings, aren't we?"

"We are. But don't you feel tired, Gwen? Like, not just trying-to-get-things-done tired, or being around for so long." He held up his hand. "It's like… we have an expiration date or something. It's as if we weren't supposed to be away from Heaven or hell for so long and we need to do something or else we will just wither away."

Now that he mentioned it, she had felt a bit off for quite a while. She had always thought it was because they were away from each other for so long. Perhaps she was wrong, and it was something else. "I suppose so."

He smiled. "But we will be opening the gates soon, and then we will be able to feel whole again. We will have all the energy we want—we won't have to take orders any longer, and we will be free to do whatever we want to each other for the end of time."

She licked her lips, wanting more than anything to be lost in James's embrace with no interruptions. But what price would that cost? And would they really be free of orders, or was that another lie?

Gwen shifted in her seat, which did not help the burning sensation in her leg. She just wanted all this to be over. She wondered if it would ever be better. For some reason deep down in her gut she knew it wouldn't be no matter who won the war. It felt like it would never change, so what was the point? The good side, or whatever they liked to call themselves, would always find some way to stop them, and they would always find a new goal to achieve. It was as if there was no end.

She felt her hands start to get a little clammy. What if there really was no end, and they were in for a series of cyclical wars and battles? What if she forever had to fight for Lucifer?

Gwen knew the answer to the last bit. Of course she would always have to fight for Lucifer—she had given her soul, or whatever theAngel equivalent was, to him. She wasn't even sure what she was anymore. Was she a fallenAngel? A demon? A vampire? Something else? Whatever it was, she doubted it would ever change no matter where she was.

James took her hand into his. "Don't worry. We will be there soon, and the pain will stop. Until we fly to our next destination."

She let out a sigh. Story of her life.

They arrived in Hong Kong and Gwen felt crowded as they made their way through the groups of people traveling from one city to the next. The gray clouds let in little light as rain poured on the glass that covered the building.

"When are we going to take over somewhere

warmer? I feel like we always go for the cold places," Gwen commented as they stepped outside to grab a taxi.

"We can spend as much time on an island, just the two of us, once this is over. I promise."

He hailed a cab, and they got in the back. James gave the driver the address that Seth had given them, and the car began to inch forward, getting through the traffic.

"Do you really believe that?" Gwen asked once they were settled.

James glanced over at her, raising an eyebrow. "I do. Otherwise, what's the point?"

So he did have doubts, Gwen thought. He just didn't let them show. "What if it isn't? What if theAngels or whoever throw something else at us? What if we will have another two-thousand-year battle to win?"

James shook his head. "There's no way—not after everything. This is it. We are almost finished."

"But that is what we said the first time. Yet here we are."

"Guinevere…"

"I'm serious, James. What if this isn't the end? What are we going to do?"

He turned to her, staring straight into Gwen's eyes.

"We fight. There isn't anything else we can do. We chose our side thousands upon thousands of years ago. There is no going back, so there is no point in wondering what we would do. We fight, Gwen. We don't have another choice."

She bit her lip. "But what if…"

"No, Gwen. I don't think you understand. If we fuck this up, that is the end. Lucifer will take you and torture you for eternity. Do you get that? Even if killing Erik brings the wrath of God or the second coming happens or we can't fulfill our mission, it won't matter. The other choice is guaranteed pain, so stop feeling sorry for these piece-of-shit apes and start caring about the demon who has sat beside you all this time, fighting for your love. Otherwise your punishment will be mine as well."

Gwen understood that—she understood that if she did anything to mess this up, it didn't mean she was the only one who would be punished but James as well. He meant the world to her, and she didn't want to see him suffer any longer.

So that was that. She had to open the gates to hell. She couldn't risk hurting James. He was her everything. He was the reason she existed—the reason she fell from

Heaven. And she would do it all over again.

It wasn't like they could run away either as Lucifer could show up in a hundred years and drag them down to hell himself. They couldn't escape—they could never be free.

Freedom was a lie, but they didn't have freedom in Heaven either, so it didn't matter. James was right. She just needed to stop thinking about it and do what she was told. Maybe then she would be happy.

And who knows, she thought, perhaps they would really get what was promised and she and James could spend the rest of eternity on some island, served by minions, enjoying the sunset every night.

The thought warmed her. What she wouldn't give to be with James fully and not have to worry about the plans for the next day. Although they liked to cause trouble and have fun, it wasn't the same as not having anything to do. The back of her mind always screamed that she needed to do something or another, and she hated that. Once this was over, there was the possibility that she was going to be able to relax.

She really doubted it, but she tried to stay positive. For James.

Gwen stared out the window as rain dripped down

from the skies. It was similar to Tokyo and yet much, much different. Tokyo, although busy and always with something to do, had moments of peace. There were parks, and nature was incorporated into the city. Hong Kong, although built between water and hills, didn't feel like that. It felt separated from the nature around it. It was a strange contrast to see.

Men and women walked to work, to a café, to see their friends or family, oblivious that a demon was passing by. The calm expressions always made Gwen want to attack them and see their fear. It wasn't just because she wanted to spread fear but to show them that she was alive and that there was much more going on in the world and they had no idea.

She had to admit she felt a bit empty inside in respect to how the world kept spinning even if she wasn't causing chaos. Even if she was, they all easily forgot about her. They dismissed her kind as fairy tales and special effects. Humans didn't believe in the supernatural even if it was right in front of their faces. It frustrated her beyond belief, but seeing the realization on their face was worth it. The pure horror and confusion was like icing on the cake.

The car stopped and James hopped out and opened

the door for Gwen. Gwen smiled. "How chivalrous."

"You know me, I used to be a knight after all."

"My dear King Arthur."

He kissed her hand. "Those were the days, weren't they?"

"That they were. It was so much easier to take over a kingdom. Now we have to make minions, and even then it is still a hassle. Back then we could just simply take the throne. It was so nice."

"Just you wait, my love. We can be the king and queen of our own little island soon enough."

Gwen grinned as they made their way into the tall building. As they stepped inside, a familiar face greeted them.

"Gwen, James. It is so nice you could join us." Seth opened his arms up like he was going to embrace her.

Gwen folded her arms in front of herself. "We came when you called. Stop acting like we are holding you up."

"I'm sorry. I'm just so used to having to wait on you I always forget. Now come. We have devised a brilliant plan, and I am dying for you to hear it."

CHAPTER SIX

A few days had passed and Christmas was over. Although the city was still busy, it was nowhere near as crowded as it was since the Christmas crowd had left, but the New Year's crowd was starting to come in. Collin couldn't believe everything that had happened within that year. It felt like a decade had passed, but it was mere months.

He couldn't imagine forever, let alone for the past couple of centuries. How could Erik and the others deal with this? How did they not go crazy?

Collin realized it was because they weren't human and were used to being alive for so long. He had no idea how much time had passed when they were in Heaven or how long Gwen and the other demons were Angels before they fell. Perhaps since they had lived for such a long time already, all this seemed like the blink of an eye.

Seeing the bags under Erik's eyes made Collin know that was far from the case.

Collin made his way through the streets of Rome, careful not to run into tourists as they pointed their cameras toward anything they could. There was a lot of history in Rome, so he couldn't blame them. If he didn't know what was coming and didn't know the truth ofAngels and demons, perhaps he too would be enjoying the sights.

He had traveled farther than he had ever thought he would in his lifetime. He had seen parts of Europe and Russian he never believed he would. Granted, it was never fun, and he didn't get to enjoy the sights, but nevertheless, he was further in life than his family ever thought he would be.

As memories began to resurface, Collin felt a chill run down his spine. No, even if they knew the truth of everything, they would think that he was worthless and not actually working. Having one's own business wasn't actual work to them. Work only included helping them out; otherwise, it was just a waste of time.

Collin kicked a pebble that was on the street. Why was he wasting his time thinking about them? They brought nothing but pain, and yet they still had some kind of hold. It wasn't fair. After everything he had been through, he shouldn't care anymore, and yet here he was, thinking about them.

They were a bunch of bastards, and he needed to let go. They had gaslighted him again and again, making him think he was the one to blame and that they were innocent. He had left them behind and moved to London, and they never came looking for him as if they assumed he would come running back to them when he failed so they could mock him. He was lucky his great aunt was there in London with him—inspiring him and motivating him to move forward with his life. She knew he'd left London and promised not to tell anyone the truth of where he went, not that they would have asked anyway.

Collin missed his great aunt. She was fun, cheerful, and spoke her mind, much like most old ladies in London he found. He never had a dull moment when she was around, and he felt like he could have some connection to his blood family with her, even if the rest hated him. Collin actually didn't think they hated him but more just didn't care about him and used him when they needed and didn't give him a second thought otherwise.

The smell of fresh bread came wafting where he was walking, and he made a quick turn to find a bakery that was open and selling bread. Although he knew it would make him a little sick and not satisfy like it would when he was human, he handed the cashier a few euros as the price for bread was rather high in Italy but definitely worth it. He didn't even wait to get back to start munching on the Tucson bread. He ripped off a piece and threw it in his mouth.

It was still warm. He smiled as he chewed. He wished he could enjoy it fully, as if he were a human, but he could not. It was said that Vlad Dracul dipped his bread in the blood of his victims, though many said that wouldn't be possible due to the fact that humans couldn't ingest that much blood. Collin wondered if Vlad was actually one of the demons or a minion. If he had to guess, he could see Jürgen as being Vlad. He had that look about him—one that meant he wasn't messing around. He shuddered at the thought.

He hadn't been hungry since Erik let him drink his blood, which was good. He didn't want to ask for more for a while. At least now he could look at humans without getting that thirst that was quite unquenchable.

It would drive anyone mad. He could see why the demons made it against the rules to make a hybrid. He wondered how long it took before the other hybrids broke—what Gwen did to make them break.

Gwen had caused Elizabeth's death through him, and that wasn't even her trying to make him break—that was just her normal darkness seeping through. He was glad she wasn't giving him much trouble as he didn't know if he could stand whatever she did to the others.

There he went again—thinking of her. He needed to stop, he knew, but she was his everything—or was. He hadn't ever loved anyone like he did her, and he knew she had loved him too. Whether she still did, he wasn't quite sure. He felt dead inside and yet still yearned for her love. He wanted to beat himself in the face with the loaf of bread and scream, "Why are you so stupid?", but he also didn't want to cause a scene.

She had betrayed him—used him—but she had let him go. She could have killed him right then and there, but she didn't. Why was that? Was it just a mistake, or had she let him go because she still felt something for him? Or was she wanting to play with him more like the others and hadn't gotten the chance? The difference he knew, however, was that the other hybrids hadn't been her boyfriends. It didn't seem like she had dated anyone except him—and James of course. James was her true love, but there was something between them. He could feel it.

He desperately needed to smack himself in the face now. He needed a distraction, and it was clear that eating the bread was not doing anything other than causing him some stomach pain.

Making his way back to the apartment they rented right outside Vatican City, Collin made his way to the top floor to find Erik making another mocha. It seemed to be his thing when he was stressed. It was fun to watch the pot sit on the stove, he guessed. It gave the mind something to focus on, even if it was for just a moment.

Collin held up the bag of bread. "Got some bread."

Erik glanced over. "Nice. Can you even stomach it though?"

He shrugged. "No, but it keeps from going insane"

"Touché. Want some coffee to go with it?"

"Sure."

He grabbed a couple of plates to serve the bread on, giving Erik a piece from the end that he hadn't bitten off. Once the coffee was done, Erik poured them both a small cup, and they sat down to enjoy the meal of sorts.

"Did you see anything fun?" Erik asked as if they were just two roommates and weren't about to go to battle with some demons.

He nodded. "Yeah, the city is beautiful."

"You were out for a while today. I take it you got lost in your mind again?"

"Yeah, well, can you blame me?"

Erik shook his head as he took a bite of the bread. "No, I can't. What is troubling you the most?"

He didn't feel like talking about his personal problems when there was so much at stake, but Erik had asked, and it was clear he wanted a distraction from it all as well, and what was a better distraction than listening to someone else's problems?

"I just keep thinking about my family. I hate them, and yet I feel bad for just leaving like that. If any of them went to the bar, they would find I was gone. I mean, they probably never went down there since they never visited anyway, but I don't know... I just feel bad. I guess it is mainly because of my great aunt. She knew I left, but I wasn't able to tell her the truth, and I feel sort of guilty."

Collin noticed Erik give him his full attention, not belittling the fact that he was talking about silly human things. Once Collin stopped talking, Erik brought his hands up in a steeple, leaning forward on his elbows.

"Why don't you go tell her the truth, or at least what you want to tell her?"

He raised an eyebrow. "You mean go back to London?"

Erik nodded. "Yes. This could be your only chance, so if you had anything you wanted to tell anyone, this possibly will be the last moment you will get to do it."

How Erik phrased that hit him like a brick wall. Was that why he was feeling so guilty? Because he knew he might die soon, and he had regrets?

"But what if the demons attack? What if I'm not here to help you?"

Erik shook his head. "Gwen will sense you went somewhere else and would wait it out. I wouldn't worry, but I would definitely wear salt just to make sure. I wouldn't want them to surround you and take you down. But if we are both careful, I think you will be all right."

"But why would you risk it?"

"I'm not. The traffic, crowds, and traveling will be jam-packed because of the holidays, so the demons won't try to move, so you have a week at least before they do anything."

That actually made sense. It would be harder for them to attack if they were constantly surrounded by tourists. I didn't think they cared about collateral damage, but flying anywhere was certainly a pain, which it would be for him as well. He didn't mind, however.

Collin nodded. "Fine. I'll do it."

CHAPTER SEVEN

James took a seat at the table next to Gwen. They were in a high-rise overlooking Hong Kong and Deep Water Bay. Sunset was almost upon them and was setting in the west on the other side of the hills. The sky was a vibrant red, even with the clouds and rains.

It was red like blood. This made James smile. He wanted more than anything to see the entire world painted in the same color.

Truthfully, he just wanted to see everything gone no matter what it was. He just wanted himself and Gwen without a worry in the world. But as Gwen said, what were the odds of that?

They were given promise after promise that they would be free to live their lives, but something always happened so they didn't actually achieve their goal. However, it didn't matter—they had to keep pushing forward, or else they would be tortured in hell for all eternity. They didn't get to be redeemed—they didn't get to change their minds like fickle humans. No, they had made their decision, and they were living with those consequences.

Just as long as they stayed alive, it was worth it. As long as they stayed out of hell, it was worth it.

Seth passed out folders. "So, the next stage of our mission?"

Gwen's hand went up before he even began to explain. He pointed at her. "You, the woman with the lying eyes and bitchy mouth. Do you have a question?"

She shot him a look, then asked her question. "Why are we in Asia when we know that Erik has been hiding in Rome? I mean, it's not like we need to take over any more governments to flush out the Gargoyles. We just have the one."

Seth pinched the bridge of his nose. "Because we could be wrong. Because something could happen, and we need to make sure we have control everywhere."

Gwen bit her lip like she wanted to pick apart his plan but decided not to. She didn't want to deal with his wrath any longer as he would just throw a fit on how her plan failed because she sabotaged it. And that was true. If it weren't for her, they would have destroyed the Gargoyles almost a century ago.

So there was no way they were going to take any crap from her.

It was nice seeing Gwen when they were back with other demons. She changed, as if the part of her mind that wanted to cause problems overrode the part of her that wanted to question everything they stood for. He could deal with the mischief—he couldn't deal with her wanting to turn her back on everything.

And everything included him.

He didn't understand how she couldn't just fake the regret as they wouldn't be together if it weren't for falling. She claimed she would do it all over again for him, but then why would she feel guilty? Why did she care so much about these idiot humans? Especially when torture awaited them both.

"Anyway," Seth went on. "In the folder are tickets to Rome. We leave in two weeks as the holidays are upon us and traveling is just a pain. There are too many humans in this world, but that will change shortly."

Although humans were a source of energy for them and something fun to play with, he couldn't wait until there were less of them around. Or at least he figured that's what would happen. Whenever there was chaos in the world or something terrifying to them, humans typically panicked and started attacking each other. They probably would not have to do a thing except show their faces, at least for a while. They also always tried to adapt to, or ignore problems. They wouldn't be able to ignore them, however.

"Two weeks, huh?" Gwen commented as she flipped through the file. She didn't seem as excited as the rest of them. She needed to act the part or else the others were going to start questioning her loyalty and possibly end her right then and there just to be safe. He couldn't let that happen.

"And then no more Gargoyles," Jürgen said. "We can finally be free of them."

"And how exactly are we going to get to Erik if he is in the confines of Vatican City? Burn Rome down again?" Gwen asked.

Seth shook his head. "No, he's not going to make us wait—not this time. He knows there is no point in hiding. This will be the battle to end the war."

"And we've been in Asia because…?"

"I already said. In case things go wrong, we have a backup. Now we have all the nations under our control so if something else throws us for a loop, we will be fine. With a snap of our fingers, the entire world will be in chaos." Seth held up his hand as if he were going to snap his fingers.

"It's so much messier now, isn't it?" Gwen sighed. "I miss the old days were we could just gain power and rule over a country. Don't you, Vlad Dracul?" She glanced over at Jürgen.

Jürgen grinned widely. "That I do, but soon we will have control over the entire world, and every human will know that we demons exist and have won the war against good and evil. That is unless you are planning on doing something stupid, in which case I will kill you."

James felt the hair on the back of his neck rise. She couldn't betray them again. He could not deal with that once more. He glanced over to her to watch her smile.

"Silly Jürgen," Gwen said. "I'm not that stupid to betray you again. Look what good it did me last time. The Gargoyles used me, betrayed me, and tried to kill me. It shows what little they care about redemption."

He pounded his fist on the table. "See, you are making it really hard for me to believe you. You are admitting if the Gargoyles had accepted you and forgiven you, you would have betrayed us all."

She kept her smile on her lips. "But that is when I would have betrayed them, just like I did in Russia. Do you not remember me using Collin, or…?"

Jürgen narrowed his eyes at her. "Which brings up another question—why didn't you kill Collin in Russia? You promised you would. I know you sensed Erik coming back for him, and yet you did nothing."

James knew he had a point. No matter how much Gwen said she would bring his end, she'd let him escape. She might have broken him—made it so he no longer trusted her—but it was clear that she let him go. They couldn't play games anymore, nor risk winning. With Collin still in the cards, Erik would be able to know when they were coming.

"He is just a human. He won't be able to hurt us," Gwen whispered.

This time it was James's turn to slam his fist on the table. "He is not just some human! If he were just some human, then you would have let me kill him years ago!"

The room was silent. Although he and Gwen fought, it usually wasn't in front of others like this. She didn't answer him, knowing that he was right.

Seth interjected. "Because we can't completely trust you at the moment, you will be confined to this building unless accompanied by one of us. You will only be filled in on details that are necessary, and James will get the rest to make sure you are in the spot you need to be."

Gwen shook her head, her eyes like daggers at Seth. "I am the one who brought Elizabeth down."

"And you are the reason Darrell is in hell. Have I made myself clear?"

She held his glare for a moment. "Fine."

Seth nodded toward the minions. "Escort Gwen to her quarters while we finish talking."

Gwen stood up and followed the minion to wherever she would be staying. Now the attention was all on James.

Seth leaned forward. "James, do you have any reason to doubt Gwen for this mission?"

James shook his head. "No, I don't see how she could sabotage it."

"But did you think she would last time?"

James shook his head again. "No, I didn't see it coming back then either."

Jürgen folded his arms in front of himself. "So we have no way of knowing what is really going on in her head."

Seth interjected. "Other than she let Collin go. If that is any indication, she is still trying to help them."

James frowned. He hated that human. He wanted more than anything to tear him limb from limb and watch him die again. But then Gwen would be sad, and he didn't want to piss her off more than she already was. "She did take down Elizabeth. I don't think if she were going to betray us again that she would do that."

"But perhaps now she realizes, oh shit, they are going to succeed."

"She has everything to lose and nothing to gain if she betrays us again," James growled through a clenched jaw. "Trust me to take care of her."

"I don't. And I won't. She doesn't get any of the information until it is deemed necessary. You are to watch her like a hawk, James. Do I make myself clear?"

James gave a sarcastic smile. "Whatever you say, Seth."

"Good. We will go over the details in the next few days. Meanwhile, make yourself at home in Hong Kong. One of the minions can show you to your room where Gwen is waiting."

James got up, and sure enough a minion was ready to take him. The minion led him to the elevator, and they went down a few levels before revealing the hotel part of the building. They passed a few rooms until the minion stopped at a room.

"This is your room, sir. Here is your key." The man bowed and left James to deal with the mess that would be inside. With a sigh, he opened the door.

Gwen was sitting on the couch, arms crossed, scowling.

"I am not some child they can just keep out of the loop."

James pinched the bridge of his nose. "No, but you are someone who betrayed us, and now the others want to keep you at a distance to make sure."

"But I'm the one who killed Elizabeth! I'm the one —"

"Do you know what it was like while you were gone? Hmm?" James yelled. "Do you know how much shit I had to take for you because I spent day after day, year after year, decade after decade searching for you? Swearing that I would make you stay in line if they just gave me a chance? Do you have any idea how much trouble you put me in with your actions, or have you always been a selfish bitch and left me to pick up the pieces?"

She didn't say anything as he went on.

"Guinevere, I love you. I would destroy this world for you. I destroyed myself for you. But we have to finish this. There is no turning back—there is no redemption. Just promise me you will do what you are told and stop arguing with Seth. He is doing his best not to kill you."

She looked away. "I'm sorry. I'll do what I am told, I promise."

He took a seat next to her and kissed the side of her head. "Thank you."

But deep down, he felt the promise was empty and that there was still something on her mind. He just hoped that, whatever it was, it wouldn't be something stupid.

CHAPTER EIGHT

Collin was gone, and Erik was left alone in the city of Rome.

He had worked missions by himself, especially after their numbers decreased with time, but today he felt truly alone. The apartment was quiet. There was no one coming. There was no one to talk to. This was the first time he had ever felt like this.

Erik knew he wasn't truly alone, as God was with him and he could communicate with the Archangels if he needed, but none of them would give him the answers he wanted. He had to figure this all out on his own, and he didn't know where to start.

He gave it only a couple of weeks before the demons would attack. Would they start the city on fire again to burn him out? Would they just start killing people until he gave in? Or would they just simply wait and know that he would come out as he had nowhere to run? No matter the situation, it was going to be a battle in the middle of this city, and there was going to be damage. Erik wanted to move—to go out in the countryside—but what was the point? He was going to lose, and all these people would be tortured or killed under Lucifer's reign anyway. It was better that he just stay where he could move between the salt line and cause problems for them.

Who knows? Erik thought. Maybe with enough patience he could win.

If Erik and Collin could weave back and forth in the salt line, not letting them deter him by torturing humans or whatever they had in store for him, if he just took it slowly and knocked them out one by one, perhaps he could win.

It was worth a shot, and it was the only way they would win.

Erik stepped outside the apartment and made his way down to the ground level. The doorman nodded to him, and Erik did the same. Out on the street, the after-Christmas crowd made their way through the businesses, spending money they'd received for the holiday or simply wanting to shop for themselves after having to buy for others. There were cafés full of humans, music stores, clothing stores, and everything humans had created. Everyone appeared to be at ease, as if the end wasn't coming.

Could they not feel it? Could they not see the chaos that all the countries seemed to be in? Or was that something they felt was normal?

Erik decided humans made no sense to him. One part of the world could be facing complete and utter chaos, but the rest would move on as if nothing were happening. When there wasn't much communication between countries, that made sense, but now that information was just a click away, and it didn't seem like that had changed.

As he debated human empathy, he made his way toward the Vatican. Although he knew that he wouldn't get any answers, he wanted to hear another Heavenly being's voice before he went into the last battle. He also wanted to make sure the church was ready for the possibility that Erik would lose. They prayed that he would win and that God had a plan, and although Erik believed God had a plan, he wasn't sure if it involved him winning.

He stepped across the salt circle, and everything felt right with the world again. It was almost as if, even though the demons were not close, all evil was vanquished from the area. He made his way through Saint Peter's Square, around the Basilica, and toward where only the higher officials were allowed to go. Erik's heart ached with memories of coming here with his colleagues—his friends—who would cause trouble, mainly Hugo. There had been more than one occasion when he used his wings and made them visible for humans to see. Luckily that was before smart phones, and the old quality of flip phones made the image blurry and no one believed it.

Although it made his heart ache, it also made his face smile. Demons weren't the only ones who had a little fun at the humans' expense. Granted, their fun and demons' fun were two completely different things. When they scared humans, it reassured their belief in God. When the demons did it, it was more to watch them scream in horror, although they sometimes repented and prayed to God. It wasn't the same, though.

Far from it.

None of the guards, cardinals, or bishops questioned his presence as he made his way down the steps of the library—where no one was permitted to go unless they had a high clearance. There were archives and relics this low in the basement that weren't for the public eye, mainly because they were fragile. Erik didn't care about them for a few reasons. First off, anything a human wrote was generally skewed by their worldview and intentions, and because he already knew it all—he had lived it.

He wasn't down here to look around at documents, however, but to get access to the tunnel that led to the room meant for the Gargoyles—or Angels, as they called them. Of anyone, they should have understood that Erik wasn't an Angel but a different Heavenly being altogether, but they didn't seem to understand. He let it go finally. No one on Earth would understand Heavenly matters.

And the demons called them Gargoyles to be annoying.

Erik sighed. He remembered the day that Gwen made the term, back in the thirteenth century when they were in France, battling. She saw a new church that was going in had grotesque statues as the drain spouts, and they were also creatures that were said to protect the church, so she decided the term fit for them. It was also to call them ugly and vile.

The thought of Gwen made his stomach turn. Had she really tried to help them, or had it been all a show to get close to Erik and the others? He still wasn't sure, and he wasn't sure if he should have ever let her near. Had it been worth transforming Collin? Granted, he would have died, and Erik liked the boy, but after everything was said and done, was he really that much of a help?

Only time would tell, he decided. And that time was coming soon.

Erik would have to give the human instructions in case he fell. He would have to go to where the gate could open and defend it with his dying breath. It would be the only thing he could do, as in Rome they were able to hide, but they wouldn't need Collin to open the gates and would just leave him behind if need be.

But hopefully it wouldn't come to that, Erik thought. He would defeat all four demons, and good would prevail.

Erik rounded a corner, and a lone cardinal stood

guard at the room he was looking for. Erik bowed his head. "Cardinal Jonathan. I am glad to see you are well."

The elderly man stood up and brushed his clothing. "Erik, I didn't know you were coming in today. No need to bow. You are much too important to bow to a lowly cardinal like me."

Erik chuckled. "You are too modest. You have an important job here at the Vatican—you keep the candles lit and make sure everyone knows how many of us are left."

The man blushed a little. "Thank you. You are too kind."

"But I suppose it is only one candle now," Erik commented.

"And hopefully I will never have to extinguish that flame."

Erik nodded, but it was a little half-hearted. He knew his time would come, and he sort of deep down wished for it. He was tired of this world and wanted to go home. "May I go in and talk to my brothers and sisters?"

"Of course. Use the room as long as you like."

"Thank you."

Erik stepped inside. It was the same as it had been for centuries. It was a simple room, in contrast to many of the other features of the Vatican. There were paintings of all twelve Gargoyles surrounding the room. There was Elizabeth and Hugo, Akira, Izel, Khalid, Zhao, Luciano, Anastasia, Maja, Arjun, and Maria. He stared at each and every one of them, remembering their time together and the promise they made to God that they would not let the demons open the gates to hell. Never could they have imagined that they would lose this war. And it would all be up to him.

One candle lit up the room, flickering shadows, making it almost appear as if the twelve paintings were moving. It smelled of wax, as the candle didn't possess a scent. Around the one lit candle were eleven that had been extinguished, never replaced, and all at different heights.

Erik knelt down in front of the candle and closed his eyes. He could still see the light—appearing red through his eyelids. He took a deep breath and waited for the calmness to come. It would be as if everything around him disappeared and only light existed. There would be no world, no evil, no darkness—it would only be goodness.

He breathed in and out slowly, waiting for an Archangel to come and talk with him, but thus far he didn't feel the tug to the other plane. He began to reach out himself but didn't hear or feel anything.

"Michael, Uriel, Gabriel, are any of you out there?" Erik whispered.

There was no response. Erik felt a sickening feeling in his stomach. "Is anyone there?"

More silence. Erik could feel his heart race. Had they abandoned him? Had they turned their backs on him because they knew he was going to fail? As he began to lose all hope, he felt something.

"Erik?" He heard a voice say. He focused and realized it was Elizabeth.

"Elizabeth? Where are the others? Why was my prayer not answered?"

"Don't worry, Erik. It isn't because they have turned their backs on you."

"Then why did they not show?"

"Because you have come here many times—because there is nothing more they can say. They feel they have failed you and that you are in this circumstance because of them."

Erik frowned. That wasn't true—far from it. It was

the demons who put him in this position. "It is good to hear your voice. I have missed you in these past few weeks."

"And I have missed you. We all have, Erik. Everyone is here, and we are waiting for you."

He should have been happy that they awaited his return, but it made him feel more alone than ever. "I don't know what to do, Elizabeth. I feel alone—I feel as if the entire war is now on my shoulders. I don't know what to do."

"It is okay to fail, Erik. Remember that. Remember no matter what evil does, there will always be balance."

"So there is something that will happen if I die? Someone who will take over?"

"Who knows? Only our God knows that."

That was true. None of us knew the outcome of anything. When we saw the Son die, we had thought it was the end back then as well. "Then what can you tell me?"

"Have hope. And trust that good will shine even in the darkness."

CHAPTER NINE

Blood covered everything. Gwen stared down at her hands to find she too was covered with the blood of the innocent. Normally this would make her feel fueled and ready to do anything, but it was the opposite. With every drop of blood came the memories of all the cruel things she had done to these humans—with every drop she could see and feel their horror. It felt as if knives were cutting into her, slicing her up, gouging her eyes out. She screamed.

The whispers of all those she killed began to get louder and louder, surrounding her and engulfing her with their words. "You did this. You are a monster. You deserve to be tortured for eternity."

The words repeated over and over again, and Gwen couldn't tell which way they were coming from. They surrounded her—suffocated her—and she screamed again.

"Please! Someone! Help me!"

But there was no one who would help her. She couldn't be saved—she couldn't be redeemed. She would simply be swallowed by the blood she spilled.

"No more," she yelled. "I can't take this anymore!"

She woke to find herself in the hotel bed. The shower was running, which she assumed was James. She rolled to face his side. Sure enough, he was gone.

Gwen was glad, however, as then she could cry a bit before he stepped out of the shower.

These dreams had been on repeat since she could remember. None of the other demons had such dreams, as she had asked long ago. She made it seem like she didn't either but had heard humans speaking of such things, but they more than likely put two and two together after she had run away.

She didn't want to get up. What was the point? She couldn't do anything alone without the others thinking she was going to betray them. She couldn't blame them, as she had betrayed them, and that feeling of regret still haunted her. She didn't understand why she was the only one who felt this way—and why she was haunted by all the blood she had spilled.

At first, she figured the more blood she spilled, the less loud those dreams would be. It was why she was known to be the most ruthless. But as the years passed, she found that it only made it worse and worse until she snapped.

But she had promised James she wouldn't betray him again. She swore that after what the Gargoyles did to her—how they just used her to get to Collin—she wouldn't want to help them. And she didn't, per se. She just wanted the dreams to go away. She wanted to clean her hands of all this blood.

She didn't know whether stopping the others from opening the gate would make all the nightmares go away, however, not to mention whatever Lucifer had waiting for her would probably be worse. She didn't know what to do.

The shower stopped, and a few moments later, James came out, a towel wrapped around his waist.

"Hey, sleepyhead, are you awake?"

Before I turned to him, I wiped away the tears and

turned to him. "That I am. Anything on the agenda that I'm allowed to do today?"

"We have a few more days before we leave. I figured you would want to go hit up the sights or something."

"In the winter?"

"It's not that cold here—not compared to everywhere else we have been in the past couple of months."

"That's true. I guess we can go somewhere."

James sat next to her and moved a strand of her hair out of her face. "Let's go out in the wilderness."

She raised an eyebrow. "You want to go hiking?"

"We used to terrorize the woods throughout the world, bringing out myths and legends all across the nations. Don't you miss getting out of where the humans are and just enjoying this world?"

She bit her lip. Perhaps that was what she needed—perhaps getting out of the places humans were would help her spirit.

"Let me take a shower and get changed."

James got them a car, and they made their way out of the city. Gwen watched as trees passed by, standing tall and not thinking of anything except growing and being. She wished she could be a tree and not have to worry about Lucifer torturing her for an eternity. Life would be so much less complicated. It sounded nice.

The two of them didn't say much. Other than traveling to Tokyo, they hadn't much time alone like this—outside the bedroom, that was. That was mainly because she had disappeared for a few decades, and before that they were planning a battle to end all battles. James was right. She did miss living in the woods and scaring any human that set foot there. When it was the two of them, she didn't second-guess herself. She was with James, and that was all that mattered.

James drove for over an hour and finally stopped the car in the middle of the woods. Even though Hong Kong was typically busy, including the surrounding areas, he had found a place that was either abandoned, private land, or did something so that no one was out there. Gwen got out of the car and stretched.

"It's actually a pretty good day to hike. The sky is clear, no people, and the air smells fresh for once."

"See, I knew this was what you needed."

"You know me all too well." She winked at him. "So, what treasures are we hiking to today?"

"There is a waterfall not too far from here. I figured we could have a picnic. I brought some cheese and wine."

"So fancy," she teased but knew it sounded good, even if they didn't need food. Alcohol helped blood cravings, but it only could do so much. It did give them a nice buzz but made them more energetic, like caffeine. She was never sure why that was but didn't question it. It was like catnip, and it was great.

They began hiking through the jungle. Creatures seemed to give them a wide birth, as if their intuition was to stay away. Typically most animals left them alone, knowing they weren't good. Except cats. Cats never seemed to care, which had to do with why Seth was so afraid of them.

Gwen could hear the birds in the distance and animals that shuffled away from them. She assumed at least one monkey, if not a group of them, ran off when they heard them coming. There was something great about creatures fearing them. If only humans still had their natural instincts—it would make everything more interesting. But no, humans ignored any intuition they had, thinking they could outwit a situation. That was never the case.

"So, are the others ever going to tell me what the plan is for when we get to Rome?" Gwen asked.

James shrugged. "I suppose, when you get there and we are about to attack."

So no. They were just going to hope James guided her in the right direction. "Do you know the plan?"

"Yup."

"Are you going to tell me?"

"Nope. The others would kill me if they found out."

That was fair. "Well, if I screw up, it's all in your hands. Don't come crying to me when Lucifer condemns you all."

"I think we are all way past that point."

She knew that was true as Lucifer had made that very clear in his last visit. She let out an audible sigh.

"What was that for?"

"Oh, nothing. Just that I feel like a little kid having to be watched constantly."

"Well, that's what happens when someone runs off and tries to destroy plans," James remarked.

"I suppose. But I feel I have already showed my worth."

"That's the problem though, Gwen. You are good at putting up a front until the last possible moment. I've seen it time and time again, Guinevere. You do it to everyone. Human, Gargoyles, demons, probably yourself."

Gwen frowned. "What is that supposed to mean?"

"You are a liar, and nothing will change that. I can't change that, but I can do things to make sure you don't screw me over."

"You think I want to screw you over?"

"Don't act like you are innocent, Gwen. You messed me up really good. I trusted you and loved you with all my heart. I still do, and that is why we are out here together. I want to show you what life will be like when we succeed."

Gwen didn't like the fact that she indeed had messed him up. She loved him more than life itself. He was the only reason she hadn't snapped. If it had just been her life on the line, then perhaps she would have already destroyed the other demons. Or perhaps, since she fell for love and not power, she would have been more evil without James. It was hard to say.

As they stepped into a small clearing, Gwen gasped. There was a small beautiful waterfall. It was the perfect temperature out, not too hot where being in the sun was burning, but not too cold where she was shaking her fist at orb in the sky. It was perfect.

"Now, shall we eat?" James asked as he took off his

backpack.

Gwen nodded as she helped him set up the picnic. James brought quite a few treats, more than he was acting like.

"This is practically a feast, James."

"What can I say? I miss our little dates."

She couldn't argue. When she was in hiding, she missed him more than he would ever know. There were many times that she had almost given up just to go back and be with him.

They munched on some of the cheese and fruit that James had brought. James took out two glasses and poured the wine.

"Oh, a nice pinot. You shouldn't have," she commented as she took a sip.

"It is a favorite. Besides, it's perfect for a day like this."

The smooth red liquid tantalized her tongue. She took a deep breath, wishing today would last forever.

And perhaps it could. James had a point—if they won, they could find some place and just live their eternity, not having a care in the world. But would that really be their reality, or would it be one thing after another ordered of them?

James leaned over and kissed her, every second becoming a little rougher. She wrapped her arms around him, pulling him closer to him. He backed off a second to whisper, "This will be our eternity."

With that, he bit into her neck, and she knew that he would always be her everything, and she must fight to protect that.

CHAPTER TEN

Collin stepped out of the plane and into Heathrow Airport. It hadn't been that long since he'd left London, and yet it felt like forever since he had been home.

It wasn't quite home yet, however, as he would need to take the Piccadilly line over to South Kensington. There he could walk over to where his great aunt Claire lived. She hopefully would be home as it was just about dinner time.

After customs, he got onto the underground and stood against one of the bars. He didn't have any luggage as he really didn't need anything. It was a quick in and out, and then he would head back to Rome without any regrets. That is if he didn't decide to go visit the rest of his family.

He really didn't want to and hoped that they all would just continue living their lives without him. He was afraid if he did go back home, they would guilt him into staying, which he couldn't as the world needed him. At least that was what Collin believed. He needed to help Erik destroy the demons so that evil wouldn't prevail.

And when Gwen died, he would die. And if the demons won, he would probably die.

So there was no way he was getting out of this alive. That was why Erik pushed him to come out here. Right.

Once they left the airport, Collin watched as rain hit the windows and could see the dreary sky engulf the land. He was definitely home now. Although it wasn't the best weather, he missed the warmness that his pub once brought people during this time of year. It used to be loud inside as men and women watched football games and rugby. He missed Hywel and his silliness and wondered how he was doing with the pub. He pondered if he should go check or not. He would decide once he got there.

Forty minutes passed, and he found himself at the

South Kensington exit. He took a deep breath as climbed up the stairs.

He was home. It felt so surreal. He was by himself— no Gargoyles, no demons, just him. He watched as Londoners, tourists, businessmen, and everything in between walked around, heading to whatever destination they needed. It wasn't quite as busy as Rome was, but it was pretty close.

Part of him wanted to turn around and head back as if this was a mistake. He didn't know if he had the courage to face his aunt and then go back to the chaos that was his new life. But Erik needed him, so no matter how hard it was, he would be able to do it.

He made his way through the winding streets and toward where his aunt lived. It was strange how crowded one street of London could be, and after you turned, it could be dead silent. Collin passed the familiar houses, glancing each way for a familiar face, but there were none.

Collin made it to his aunt's little cottage. The light was on inside, so he slowly knocked at the door.

"One moment!" Aunt Claire called from wherever she was in her home. A few seconds later, the door opened.

Collin smiled down at his aunt as she looked up at him, her eyes still sparkling like they did in old photos. She grinned.

"Collin! My dear boy! Come in, come in!"

He stepped inside, and the air brought back fond memories. It smelled of bread and roses. He wished he could capture the scent and take it wherever he went.

Trinkets covered all the tables and trays. He noticed there were more than when he left, which made him smile. He wondered if they were gifts or if she had gone out and got some.

"Would you like some tea and cookies?" She asked.

He nodded. "That would be wonderful. Do you need help?"

She shook her head, her white curls unmoving as if she had sprayed an entire can of hair spray on them. "No, no. Take a seat. I can tell you traveled far to get here."

Collin sat down on the green plastic-covered couch and stared down at the shaggy carpet. Some things never changed.

"Now, tell me what you have been up to, boy," she said as she brought in the teapot, her hands shaking. He took in a deep breath, wanting to grab it from her but knowing she would scold him.

"Away. Traveling. That sort of thing."

She went back and grabbed a couple of teacups. "That sounds lovely. You got to see the world you always wanted."

Well, sort of. "Yeah, it was nice seeing different countries."

"And what of the girl?"

He frowned. How could he explain Gwen to her? "We are having some troubles."

"You have to listen to women, sweetie. Don't be a typical man and not listen to what she has to say."

The problem was definitely not me listening to her. The problem was I listened to her too much, but that wasn't going to be easy to explain. "I will try."

"Are you going to go after her?"

Not in the way she was suggesting, Collin thought to himself. "Yes, she will be in Rome, and I am… going to corner her there."

"Oh, you are leaving so soon again?"

"Yes, I wanted to come back and tell you… I might not be coming home again. I… We… She and I are going to run away to a different country. Her home country, actually. It's pretty far, and travel will be expensive." That wasn't a complete lie. If I died, I would be going to her home.

She poured some milk in each of our cups and two sugar cubes. She started to pour the tea. "Well, I will miss you. And if anyone asks, I will say you eloped and have run away like you always dreamed."

Collin smiled as he blew on his tea. "Thank you, Auntie. I feel bad."

"What for?"

"Because I am leaving you alone here, and because… well… I'm not saying goodbye to the others."

Aunt Claire set her teacup down. "Don't you dare be unhappy because of those twits. They have done nothing with their lives, and the moment you started wanting to explore and do something more, they gaslighted you. Don't you dare let them ruin your happiness. Be who you want to be. And I'm not alone here. I have friends and some family visits. I'm happy here, and I want you to be happy as well."

Collin tried not to tear up, but felt droplets escape his eyes. She was right. They did want to control him to ruin his happiness. He had known that again and again but couldn't help but think of them. He needed to let go of the past and move forward.

Not that he had much forward left to go, as he doubted he would be alive much longer.

"Thank you, Auntie. I love you and appreciate you. You know that?"

She grinned ear to ear. "Of course. I'm the best aunt around."

They finished their tea and cookies, and Collin knew he needed to head back. There was only so much time, and he didn't know if he could only spend one night there without wanting to stay forever.

As he headed back to the station, he realized he did want to check out the pub just to see if Hywel had it covered. It was his dream to open a pub, and even though he wouldn't be coming back, seeing if it survived would be good enough for him.

Collin headed south into Chelsea, clutching his coat to stay warm. It was evening now, and it was getting a bit chilly, especially with the sprinkling of rain. He rounded a few more corners and found that he was in front of his bar—Lancelot's.

It was still intact, which was a good sign. He stepped through the door and found it as lively as ever. It wasn't so packed that he couldn't find a spot at the bar, but there was a decent number of people. As he took a seat, a familiar bartender came to great him.

"Collin! Bloody hell, it's you!" Hywel exclaimed as he came around the bar and picked him up in a hug.

Collin felt the air leave his lungs as the tall Welsh man squeezed him tight. Finally he was free. "How are you doing? How is business?"

"It is good. Everything has been running smoothly. It takes a lot of work to run this place, but I got it under control. But what about you? What have you been up to? Are you coming back for good?"

Collin spilled briefly. "I'm fine. No, I wanted to visit real quick. Just here for the day. I wanted to check in on you all and see how the business is going."

"Fine? That's it? You left for a girl, and you just say fine? Come on, give me the details."

Collin watched as the eyes of this former employee sparkled. His face was still scruffy, and his red-blond hair was messy. Some things never changed. "We had a hiccup, but I am going to corner her in Rome, and we are going to run away to her home country."

His eyes widened. "So you are going to be gone forever? Part of me had hoped you would eventually come back. I kept some of your stuff for you if you did. Do you want to look through it?"

Collin glanced up at his old bedroom. He had completely forgotten he left most of his belongings here. Was there anything he really wanted to keep though? Would it even matter?

He finally shook his head. "Nah. Where I am going, it won't benefit me. Feel free to keep it or sell it."

"So I can have your wicked swords?" Hywel's blue eyes practically twinkled.

Collin laughed as he nodded. "Of course. It's not like they let you on the plane with those anyway." At least not without the Gargoyles' help. They could convince a human to do anything, which came in handy.

"Well, tell me. How have you been?"

That was a good question. He had seen and done things no human ever thought possible. "I have been all right. Life has been an adventure these past few months, and I never thought any of it would happen. I've traveled a good part of Europe and Russian."

"So, what did you do to screw it up with the girl?"

Collin sighed. "Why does everyone assume I screwed it up? Perhaps she crossed me?"

Hywel raised an eyebrow. "Oh? Did she now?"

He wasn't having it. This made Collin laugh, missing the times he'd had with Hywel. They ended up talking for hours as the other waiters and waitresses took over Hywel's position. If Collin could do it all over again, he wondered if he would have still tried to run away with Gwen the first time, before he knew what she was.

CHAPTER ELEVEN

James glanced at his watch. They were to leave within a few days, and the battle to end all battles would begin. He took a deep breath as he peered out the window of his hotel room. Gwen was still asleep as she always hated mornings. He couldn't blame her, especially since they spent most of the night awake.

Their day out had proven to be quite fruitful as he could tell Gwen was still uneasy about opening the gates to hell. But after showing her a day like that—and what their life could be like—he had a feeling he had convinced her otherwise. Only time would tell, however, and he and the others were keeping a close eye on her.

The streets of Hong Kong were busy as usual. James watched as the humans went on with their day, not realizing what was truly above them—a group of demons plotting their demise. Soon all the world would be under their rule—truly. No Gargoyles would be coming to end them—no good guys having to defeat the bad guys. Hell would be leaderless and all their brethren would resume their positions of power.

And he and Gwen could disappear, never to be seen again. He couldn't wait.

They both had fallen for each other, never wanting to be apart. Hell, the most they had been away from each other was when Gwen ran off. Never had they wanted to be separated. He knew Gwen wanted to be with him, and that he wasn't the reason she ran away, but he couldn't help but feel a little bit betrayed. It hurt him as she was supposed to be his everything and he hers. And yet he wasn't enough for her, and she had found that ridiculous human.

He couldn't wait to tear him limb from limb. They were supposed to focus all their efforts on Erik, but

James knew he was going to try his best to end the wretched hybrid. If it weren't for Collin, Gwen would have come back to him sooner.

Granted, Gwen ran away way before Collin existed. James felt that Collin's love for Gwen was what made her waver so many times in the past few years. She even confessed to him that if a human could love her, even after knowing what she was, perhaps a demon could make a difference. It was that mindset that he needed to destroy more than anything.

There wasn't a doubt in James's mind that Gwen didn't love him—it was just her doubts on what would happen after they opened the gates to hell that made her waiver.

He took a deep breath and let it out slowly. It would be fine. It would all work out in the end.

His phone buzzed, and he checked it. It was Jürgen.

Meet us in the debriefing room in ten minutes. Don't bring Gwen.

James sighed. The question was, did he wake her up and tell her where he was going, or did he leave her here to sleep and hopefully not wake up before he was back? Minions were at the door, making sure she didn't leave, but they could only do so much if she really wanted to get away. The odds were that she wasn't going to go anywhere as he doubted Collin and Erik would believe anything she had to say after how she killed Elizabeth.

He left her sleeping. She was tired, as was he. It was as if something was draped over him at all times and he was trying to move through an ocean. It didn't used to be like this, and he had noticed it slowly in the past centuries. After Gwen left him, it became more and more prevalent. He had always thought it was because he needed her blood, but apparently that wasn't the case.

The thought of asking Jürgen and Seth if they felt the same crossed his mind occasionally, but then he always decided not to. He didn't want to admit a weakness as that would only make matters worse. They already hated the fact that he and Gwen had a blood bond, which strengthened them when they were together but weakened them when they were apart. They might attribute this feeling to that when James knew deep down that wasn't the case. These bodies were slowly dying, and if they didn't open the gates, they would perish.

Which was never part of the deal. Lucifer forgot to

include details like that and how they needed blood to survive and all that. He also said that if they followed him that they would get to live their lives how they wanted, and that was definitely not the case. Then there was killing the Son of God and then destroying the Gargoyles.

So yes, he did understand Gwen's constant dilemma, but there was no going back, so what was the point of disobeying orders?

James stepped out of the hotel room and nodded to the minions. There were three Hong Kongers guarding the door, all of them appearing as if they belonged to some kind of gang or something. Tattoos peaked out from under their suits, and they wore shades even thought they were indoors. James caught sight of guns tucked away under their suit coats.

Yeah, definitely gangsters, James thought.

They didn't pay him much mind as he went toward the elevator and took it up to the meeting room. Most of the plan in Rome was set in stone, but he had a feeling Seth just wanted to go over it again in case they forgot. It was the simplest plan ever, so he didn't understand why he had to keep talking about it.

Other businessmen and women were in the elevator.

Most of them were minions, taking care of whatever business Seth had organized here. Seth had gone over it, but James didn't really care as it didn't concern him.

Ah, James thought, that was why Seth wanted to go over the plan again.

Jürgen and Seth were already in the room, waiting for him. James checked his watch. Only seven minutes had passed since he got the text, so he wasn't late. They were just always early to make it seem like they were waiting on him. He hated it when they did that.

"What is Gwen up to?" Seth asked as he leaned back in his chair.

James shrugged. "Sleeping. It is pretty early in the morning. I figured you were having this meeting knowing she would still be asleep and wouldn't try to run off."

"You think she would run off if she were awake?" Seth asked.

James shook his head. "No, but that is why you have guards outside our door at all times, right? Because you don't trust her."

Seth shrugged. "What can I say? Once a traitor, always a traitor."

James couldn't argue with that. "So, why did you

bring me down here this early in the morning?"

Jürgen crossed his arms in front of himself and leaned back. "We wanted to go over the plan one last time."

James sighed. "Fine. We leave in a couple of days, right? Could anything really have changed?"

Seth gestured. "Then go ahead and explain it."

James raised an eyebrow, but stated the mission. "We are going to Rome. The four of us are going to surround the Vatican and wait. The moment one of us sees movement, we shoot a flare in the sky to let the others know where Erik is. Then we surround and attack him. If we all focus on him, we will be able to take him out."

"And Collin?" Jürgen growled.

James eyed him. "We only fight if he attacks us. He isn't important for this mission unless he attacks."

"So you aren't going to go after him and jeopardize the mission?" Seth accused.

James let out a laugh. "And why would I do that?"

"Jealousy. Anger. Resentment. Those are just a few emotions that are apparent on your face. You had your chance to kill him, and you didn't because you were too afraid that Gwen would be upset and because you trusted her when she said that she would kill him in

Moscow. She didn't, and now you want to seek your revenge. Are we wrong?"

Seth wasn't wrong. James clenched his fist. "I want him dead."

"And he will be," Jürgen growled. "But we can deal with him after we deal with Erik."

"We can't have anything go wrong, James," Seth warned. "Or else we will be tortured for all eternity."

James slammed his fist on the table. "That was not what we were promised! None of this is! We were told we would be able to do whatever we wanted if we followed Lucifer!"

He shouldn't have said that. None of them could show doubt—it was like showing weakness.

Seth stood up and leaned forward on his hands that were on the table. "Are you on Gwen's side now? Do we need to take both of you out before you take us out?"

James slowly shook his head. "No. I know there isn't anything to gain by turning on Lucifer. I'm just frustrated. I promise I won't jeopardize the mission. I want all this to be over as much as you do."

Seth nodded and took a seat. "Good. We leave in three days. You better make sure your girl follows orders, or else we will end her. You got that?"

James did. It was a threat he knew all too well. "Don't worry. If she does anything to betray us, I will end her myself."

CHAPTER TWELVE

Erik could feel a change in the air. The demons were planning their attack. It was only a matter of time now.

Collin had decided to spend the night in London. Originally he was just going to go for the day and come back that night, but it seemed he got wrapped up in talking with his friends. Erik knew he wouldn't turn his back on the war, but he deep down wished that he would—he wished that Collin had been given the choice to go back to living a normal life while he could.

But what were the odds of Erik winning? He found

them to be rather low. Erik didn't trust that he was going to win by himself, but after talking with Elizabeth the day before, he wondered if it mattered. She didn't seem distraught or worried about him, but it seemed like she knew the truth of what was going to happen. He wished he knew what would happen so he could go on knowing whatever happened that it would all be fine.

Perhaps he should trust that she knew best and not worry—perhaps in his death something miraculous would happen. It didn't seem that way for the other Gargoyles, however, so he didn't think that was actually a possibility. Perhaps the Lord would appear and smite down all the demons. That would be a sight, but it was clear from the beginning that He would stay out of it all. Erik had to keep reminding himself of that.

So what else was there to do but wait? He hated waiting probably as much as the demons did. He could usually count on their impatience, but this time was different—this time it wasn't Gwen in charge, which meant they were making a backup plan. They knew as well as Erik did that something always came up, and it was possible that Lucifer had lied to them once again.

This made Erik smile. They had been lied to so many

times, as Lucifer was known as the king of lies. First, they were promised freedom in the battle of Heaven, and then when they destroyed the Son of God, and now this. He couldn't blame them for having a backup plan.

Although he was still afraid that this was the end, as it felt like it was, he needed to trust in God. Not all this was just up to him, but there was always an answer to everything. Erik took a deep breath as he sipped his coffee. He needed to trust in God. Good always found a way.

Erik wondered what he should do as he waited for Collin to be back. He felt so alone, a creature that didn't change with time, and yet the entire world kept on revolving around the sun, changed with the seasons, and humans came and went. It was disorienting to say the least. He tried to stay away from humans for just that reason—they always passed so quickly that neither Erik nor the others could really deal with it. At first, humans would help them in their fight against demons, but the more humans that teamed up with them, the more lives were lost. They felt heartache for each one even though they knew they would go to Heaven. Usually, there were some that had become corrupt by the demons before they were killed. Erik felt sorry for those souls, but there wasn't anything they could do about it.

After a few centuries, they stopped teaming up with humans in such a way. It was easier not having to worry about their lives, but the demons never stopped involving humans and killing, mainly because they could make minions that way and demons themselves had to feed. But the Gargoyles couldn't bring humans into it—not after all the lives that had been lost.

That was until Collin came into their life. Erik didn't want to involve him, but Gwen had already done so by half turning him and feeding him her blood. It was Erik, however, who made her completely turn him. He couldn't undo what he had done, however, and Collin would never have a normal life.

Deciding he needed to go outside and clear his head, Erik grabbed his coat and put on some boots. It was cool outside, not warm but not freezing either. Luckily the sky was clear, and he was able to enjoy the day. It had been a while since he got wander around Rome, as usual he only stopped by to perform the candle ceremony, and of course now he was simply waiting for the end, but he wasn't going to worry about that for the moment. No, he was going to go relish in the sights and eat good food and pretend for once that he was a normal human visiting the city.

It was past the new year, and all the festivities had now come to an end. There were still quite a few tourists using the past few days off they had to sightsee and shop and whatever humans did for fun. Erik wondered what it would be like to have work in the way that they did and only so many days to enjoy. He didn't quite understand how the world came to be that way, but it was for humans to figure out—not him.

There were many people lined up to go inside the buildings and areas the Vatican had opened for visitors. Erik debated joining them but decided he'd spent a lot of time inside there already and he would enjoy other parts of the city better.

Rome was enriched with much history—some buildings even older than he was. Or at least how old he was on Earth. He had lived for many centuries in Heaven as well—before Earth was even created. But there were a lot of things he remembered watching being built. Some of it was fond memories, and others not so much.

Erik headed east and passed the Castel Sant'Angelo. Hadrian had been an interesting emperor. They were always wary of him, not sure if he was a minion or just a human who was selfish and greedy. There were definitely many emperors who sided with the demons who didn't have to be turned into a minion. Erik was never sure why the demons let some humans just side with them when the demons knew as well as the Gargoyles that humans liked to change sides at a whim. Perhaps they liked the chaos, which was definitely possible. Or perhaps they liked to show the Gargoyles that humans were as corrupt as demons and that they didn't need saving. It was probably the latter.

He turned and stepped on the pedestrian bridge that went across the River Tiber. There were quite a few people moving across the bridge, taking pictures of both the Castel and of the natural beauty of the river. As they were distracted by taking a picture, Erik watched as two teens grabbed a man's wallet out of his back pocket and a clutch purse out of a woman's bag. After they thought themselves successful, they turned and hurried off in the direction Erik was heading. They didn't run but walked quickly, not to gain attention.

Except Erik knew what they had done, and he had nothing better to do. He followed after the two teens as they turned corner after corner. They stopped in a narrow alleyway, thinking they had successfully pickpocketed someone. As they began to flip through the wallets, Erik stepped up to them.

"How about you two give back what you stole?" Erik grinned.

The two boys jumped but saw it was only Erik. The taller one nodded to him.

"How about you walk away and forget you saw anything? We are just trying to make a living here."

Erik didn't move. "If you do the right thing, I think God will reward you."

They both laughed. "What?" the shorter of the two began. "Are you some kind of priest?"

He didn't typically do this, but since it was just the three of them, Erik thought he could have a little fun. For a moment, he let his wings appear, stretching out and taking up a good part of the alleyway. The two teens fell back, wide-eyed, and began screaming.

Erik went back to normal. "Now, what were you saying?"

"We will take it back! We will take it back!" The two scrambled to their feet and ran back toward the bridge.

Erik laughed as he kept moving forward. He knew those two would do the right thing. And hopefully this had taught them a lesson and they would turn their lives around. One could only hope.

He made his way through the city, enjoying the old buildings and history of everything around him. How long had it been since he simply walked around and enjoyed the place? There were always plans and things to do. He tried to recall the last time he took a trip to Rome to just be, but it was fuzzy. Was it in the eighteen hundreds? Or before that, during the Renaissance? Why couldn't he remember?

Time was a tricky thing. One blink and this entire area could change. A lot of European places didn't change as drastically as others, which was a shame as all the others normally changed due to war or conquest. Then once more and more humans settled into a place, their numbers drastically grew. Erik didn't know if this was a good thing or not.

He passed through the Piazza Navona. Everyone seemed to be happy, enjoying their time around the square that had been there almost as long as Erik had been on Earth. Artisans, cafés, and performers filled the area. Everyone was enjoying themselves. It was a style of life that Erik wished more humans would take up—just being in and enjoying community.

But if he didn't win, it wouldn't matter. There would be no community—no time to enjoy. He took a breath and made his way back to his apartment. Going out had been a mistake—it only made him worry even more.

CHAPTER THIRTEEN

So they really weren't going to tell her the plan. This made Gwen roll her eyes as the four of them went out for a bite to eat.

She knew it was probably something simple and not as elaborate as her plans had always been. Then again, there was only one Gargoyles left and four of them, so it wasn't like they had to trick anyone. She also always made it too complicated, and that was when something went wrong.

What she wanted to know was what they were going

to do with Collin. She shouldn't care. Hell, she should have killed him when she had the chance, but that didn't happen and now here they were with a wildcard in the mix.

But it was more fun that way, no?

Gwen knew she had promised James she would kill Collin and give James his head on a silver platter, but deep down she couldn't do it. While he would never mean what James meant to her, Collin had a part of her heart. He accepted her for who she was, flaws and all. Well, perhaps not now since she had used him to kill Elizabeth. She had told Collin that she had changed and wanted to help the Gargoyles, and because of his trust in her one of them was dead. Everyone had to admit, though, it was a really good plan, and she would like to see anyone come up with something better.

"Are we there yet? I'm hungry!" She whined.

Jürgen shot her a look. "Say that one more time, and I will drive a stake through your heart."

"Tsch, you lie."

"Go ahead and say it to find out."

She wasn't going to speak because Jürgen had every reason to hate her and want to end her life. He would have just used this as an excuse. She folded her arms in front of her as James wrapped his hand around her waist.

"Don't worry, my love. We are almost there."

She raised an eyebrow. "And how would you know that? Seth is leading the way. We probably will cross into China before he decides on a place." She said the last bit loudly so he would hear her.

Seth ignored her, which was surprising as he always liked to make a big deal out of everything. She sighed and kept following. She really was hungry and needed some blood before they made their way across the world and to Rome. Gwe n was sure they would get their fill there before they attacked, but that didn't mean she wasn't hungry at that moment.

James and she got a little bit of a fill when a hiker had wandered into their picnic and had witnessed them feeding on each other. He tried to run, but alas, he didn't get far. It had been a while since Gwen had hunted a human through the jungle. It felt fantastic and made her stop questioning some things.

This was who she truly was, and she needed to stop kidding herself. There was no redemption, and even if Lucifer had lied again, it would still be better than being tortured. At least that was what she hoped.

She did notice, however, that James was a bit anxious. Was he afraid the mission would fail? Or did he think she would actually betray him again? She wished she could reassure him that she wouldn't leave him again, but it wouldn't help. She had done it once, and there was no way to persuade him that she wouldn't do it again. It really had appeared as if she had gained a conscience out of the blue, but it was a long time coming, which she knew was probably worse to him. He thought he had known her, but she had surprised him.

Gwen knew she could never hurt him again like that. So she decided at the picnic she would push all thoughts and fears away and focus on what she loved best—James and the ecstasy she felt when consuming blood. It was how she got through all those centuries before, and she would just do it again.

They stopped in front of an inconspicuous door. Gwen raised an eyebrow. An underground club—how lovely.

She grabbed James's hand and squeezed it, giddy with excitement. He leaned over and kissed her.

"I love it when you have that smile," he said in her ear.

"The smile of I'm going to tear out a bunch of people's throats?"

He kissed her again. "Yup."

She laughed as they entered the club. Lights flashed and music was blaring loud enough where she couldn't even hear herself think. This was the perfect place to find something to eat.

Seth closed the door behind himself and busted the lock. He turned to everyone and smiled. "Well then, have at it."

They didn't even take time to dance before going after each of the fifty or so people who made up this small, intimate club. The screams were drowned out by an electric beat. Gwen grabbed the closest girl and bit into her neck, draining her of all her blood.

Gwen felt as if the hairs on her body were standing on end. There was something instinctual when the scent of blood was in the air—it was as if any reasoning or questioning was out the window and all there was left was the thirst for blood and the need for energy. It was like a high of sorts, but stronger and more animalistic. She had tried some drugs out of curiosity, but they never compared to the taste of blood on one's lips.

It was like this for every demon as she watched her

comrades ripped apart the throats of the humans that were in this club. The music kept playing, as if the DJ hadn't noticed the terror that was going on. Gwen glanced up at the staging area to find that the woman who was mixing the beat had her eyes closed as she rocked to the music she played.

Gwen's lips curled as she used her speed power to appear next to the woman. Still the woman didn't notice as she kept listening to the music. Gwen tapped her on the shoulder. The girl's eyes flickered open and peered over toward Gwen, confused for a moment. She then turned her attention to the rest of the club to find the bloodbath that was going on.

She began to scream. It was music to Gwen's ears. She wanted more than anything to listen to the sweet sound, but her hunger was stronger. Gwen grabbed the girl and bit into her neck. The red liquid filled her mouth, and the screams died off as the body went limp. She kept drinking, gaining her fill, taking all the life out of this human. As long as she completely destroyed the body, then the human wouldn't turn into a minion. It was only if they bit a human without completely destroying the body that a minion could take possession.

Gwen joined James as he held on to a man who was trying to run away and at the same time bit into a girl's throat. Gwen grabbed the man and began to feed off him. At this rate, she wouldn't need to feed in Rome. That was a lie if she ever knew one. She needed to feed in order to be at her fullest energy, especially if they were going to take down the last Gargoyles.

She still wasn't sure what was going to happen when they opened the gates to hell, if they were even actually going to open, but she knew James was right—obeying orders was better than torture. She needed to stop worrying about the damage she was doing—she needed to push all those thoughts deep down into the back of her mind and keep on moving forward. It was the only thing she could do.

Both she and James let go of the bodies, and James grabbed her and kissed her bloodstained lips. His lips also tasted of blood, and she relished in it. She wanted to be like this with him forever—she didn't care about anything else but him.

Their kiss was interrupted by gagging noises. Gwen turned to find Jürgen acting like he was sticking his finger in his throat. She rolled he r eyes.

"Grow up, Jürgen. You know that James and I can't

help but want to make out after feeding. It's intoxicating."

"It's disgusting, and you know it."

She shrugged and turned back to James to kiss him one more time. She backed away and took a look at the bodies that were on the ground. Her black boots were stepping in the pool of blood that covered the entire floor of the club. It smelled sweet and beautiful.

"Well then, are we ready to head to Rome?" Her eyes flickered over to Seth.

He grinned. "That we are. But I'm still not telling you the plan."

Gwen rolled her eyes, but she didn't really care. The end was near whether she liked it or not.

CHAPTER FOURTEEN

Collin spent the night at his old pub, lost in thought as his mind drifted back to all the old memories of living there. It felt like a lifetime had passed, but it had only been a few months. He wished he could go back to that life—taking care of customers and having a good time. But that life was no more. He had to finish this, and with it he would be forfeiting his life.

Now that the time was getting nearer, he realized he didn't want to die. The thought of sacrificing himself had seemed fine at the time, but after coming back to his old home, it made his heart race and he wanted to run. There wouldn't be a point in running, however, since he would die if Gwen died, or he would more than likely be destroyed with the rest of the world once the gates to hell were open.

So it really didn't matter.

Grabbing his backpack, which had his wallet, passport, and some extra clothes just in case, he started for the door.

"Wait," Hywel called after him. It was morning now, and he was getting the pub ready for the day. "Are you really leaving forever?"

Collin turned to him and nodded. "Yeah, I think I am."

Hywel wrapped his arms around Collin and gave him a tight hug. "I'm going to miss you, *ffrind*."

Ffrind. Friend in Welsh. Collin missed his random Welsh words. He hugged Hywel back.

"I will miss you too. But know that I am doing what I love, all right? And keep this place running. You seem to love it here."

"Indeed I do. I just wish you were here with me like old times. Sometimes I get the strangest dreams as to why you left, like with vampires and such. It's crazy.

It's like I remember someone trying to bite my neck."

So the memory wipe didn't quite work with him. But luckily, Hywel more than likely passed it off as something else entirely.

"Well, I'm no vampire," Collin lied as he showed him his teeth. "See, they aren't pointy at all."

Collin knew he could scare the poor guy and make his canines long and his eyes yellow, but he decided not to. That wouldn't be a good way to part.

"Right. You know how it is—I watch all those horror movies. They must have snuck into my dreams."

Or it in fact happened, and he was starting to remember. Collin didn't correct him but nodded. "Yeah, maybe stay away from those for a while."

"Nah, I like the adrenaline. Not all of us can run off and see the world."

And not all of us can have happy, comfortable lives, Collin thought. "Yeah, I guess not."

"Well, you give your girl a kiss for me. After you make up, of course. It would be weird if you kissed her before that."

Collin wanted more than anything to confess everything to Hywel about what had happened. He needed someone's opinion on what he should do and one who wasn't from Heaven. But he couldn't do that because Hywel would think he was crazy, and he didn't want anyone else to have the burden of knowing the truth.

"I will. And you take care, okay? I will miss you."

Hywel gave him another hug, and he turned to leave this world behind for good.

The flight was rather comfortable. He was able to upgrade to business class and had nice leg room and drinks. He had a glass of scotch and did his best not to have a panic attack. This could be his last flight—this could be his last few days.

He needed to stop thinking about it. He had almost died quite a few times before, so why was it bothering him so much now?

Collin wasn't sure of the answer. Perhaps he had always believed that Gwen would be redeemed and they could live out their lives together. After what had happened in Moscow, he knew that wasn't going to be a possibility.

After the two-and-a-half-hour flight was finished, the plane landed, and he walked through the Rome airport and grabbed a taxi to take him back to where the apartment was. It was a good twenty minutes back to Vatican City from Leonardo di Vinci Airport, and the apartment was right outside the Vatican.

It was strange being so close to a holy city, or at least where the pope lived. Collin didn't exactly understand why people put so much faith in a human to tell them what to do instead of just believing in themselves. From what Collin could tell, no human was holier than another, but all had the ability to commune with God.

He was in a different boat, however, as he got to interact with the Gargoyles and knew exactly what was going on with the war between Heaven and hell, or at least mostly. Even Erik wasn't sure what was going to happen, which didn't help his faith in what they were doing. Would good reign as it always did, or would evil finally have its chance?

The cab passed by the outskirts of Rome, which appeared similar to the countryside of England other than being a lot sunnier. There were a lot of fields and small homes and greenery. Sure, the plants appeared different, but it had that quiet, natural feeling that Collin wished he could enjoy more.

Twenty minutes passed, and they were now in the more crowded part of Rome. The cab was a few blocks from the apartment but stuck in traffic as there wasn't a lot of road space in the city center. Collin handed the driver the euros and got out of the car to walk the rest of the way. It was more than likely faster, and Collin didn't want to be cooped up any longer.

Life was going on per usual as the people of Rome went about their business. Collin jammed his fists in his jacket pockets and kept his head down. He didn't want to be around humans anymore—not now that he was different. Not now that he had seen so many of them ripped apart by demons.

Erik was in the apartment already, sipping on a mocha. This made Collin smile as it seemed to be the only thing that relaxed the Gargoyles.

"I'm back," Collin said as if it wasn't apparent.

"How was your trip? Were you able to say all the goodbyes you wanted?"

Collin nodded. "Yeah. I saw my auntie and went back to my pub to see how it was. Seems Hywel has things under control, which surprised me, but I am glad."

"That's good," Erik commented, but it seemed like his mind was somewhere else.

Collin collapsed in the chair opposite to him. "I just wish it was still my home, you know?"

Erik nodded. "And I am sorry that it isn't. The demons have destroyed many people's lives, and it breaks my heart seeing it every time."

Collin could see the truth in his eyes when he said that. He wondered how many times he had watched a human suffer because of the demons. It had been James's fault that he was like this as James had almost killed him. It was only because Gwen loved him at the time that he was still alive. He should have been dead.

And if he had died that night, his pub would have never opened, he would have never have befriended Hywel, and he would have never had to know the truth about Angels and demons. But he also wouldn't have had to know the horrors of watching humans be slaughtered—and crave their blood as he watched them die.

No, he wouldn't wish this upon anyone else, although he knew that it indeed had happened to others, and that was why the demons weren't supposed to make hybrids ever again. He wondered what exactly happened with those hybrids and how much different they were than him.

"Anything interesting happen here?" Collin asked Erik.

Erik shook his head. "Nothing different than usual."

Collin stood up. "Well, I guess that is good. I am going to take a nice, long hot shower and we can plan exactly what we are going to do." That was when he felt it—the demons were moving.

"What is it?" Erik asked.

"They are coming."

CHAPTER
FIFTEEN

James couldn't believe that not even he was trusted for when they were actually leaving. It was two days earlier than the tickets Jürgen and Seth had given Gwen and him. He understood why, but that didn't mean that he wasn't a bit pissed. They had no reason not to trust him, and yet here he was—caught off guard.

He let it go. There was no point in arguing now, especially since they were already on the plane. James shifted in his first-class seat. His ankle burned, and he kept checking his pants to make sure they wouldn't catch fire. It had never happened, as it wasn't an actual flame, but it sure felt like it.

Gwen leaned over and whispered in his ear. "I told you we need to destroy all planes when we rule. Then we won't have to burn ever again."

He smiled. "Yeah, well, soon, my love. Soon."

The flight attendant came over. She was younger with dark brown hair and a short stature. "Would you two like anything to drink?"

Gwen answered. "Wine, please."

"Whiskey. Scotch, if you have it," James said.

The flight attendant bowed and went off to grab their drinks. Jürgen and Seth were on the other sideof first class, which James appreciated as he didn't want to deal with their comments. Seth probably did it on purpose.

The flight attendant brought their drinks, and Gwen took a big gulp of the wine.

"Whoa there," James commented as he took a sip of his whiskey. It was Laphroaig, one of his favorites. "Don't want to get drunk on the plane."

She laughed. "As if I could get drunk on some wine."

He leaned in to whisper in her ear. "I could add a couple of drops of blood to give it some effect."

Gwen might have rolled her eyes at the comment, but

he saw the smile on her lips. "Knock it off. We don't need panic on a plane."

"Oh, come on. Wouldn't it be fun?"

She shook her head. "No because we can't fly a plane. And because Seth or Jürgen, probably Jürgen, would kill you."

"Where is that girl who used to cut off her arm and put it back to scare townsfolk?" James jested.

She turned to face him, sipping her wine. "Wishing she was on land so she could do just that."

He laughed. "Fair enough. Being in the sky isn't fun and games, is it? We need to get back to the ground and cause some chaos."

"Which we will, dear, in due time."

He stroked his finger on her cheek and chin. "No, I'm not giving you the details."

She let out a playful laugh. "That's fine. I can cause more chaos without knowing. I'm not sure what Seth is thinking by keeping me out of the loop."

"He probably just wants you to feel like a child who is in trouble. Because you are."

She shot him a look. "Hey, watch your tongue. Besides, the things that I do to you definitely make me not a child."

He grabbed her hand and kissed it. "That is definitely true. But I can't tell you. Those two might not act like it, but we know perfectly well they can hear us."

James's eyes moved toward Jürgen and Seth. Jürgen turned and glared at him. James gave Gwen another kiss on her hand.

"So sit tight, my love. We will be there soon, and then paradise will await us."

Gwen took back her hand and grabbed her drink, sipping it as she peered out the window. "A paradise with no planes. I can't wait."

They arrived at Leonardo di Vinci Airport fifteen hours later. James stretched as he peered up at the darkening sky. It was good to be back in Rome. It had been so long. Since the Holy Roman Empire, they tended to stay away from the area, which really was unfortunate as it was such a beautiful place with great food, both cuisine and the blood. There had been so many sacrifices in this country given to them. The Roman Empire was a wonderful time that James wished he could go back to.

But time moved on, and so did they. After this was over with, they could find their places and forget about it all. That is, if Lucifer kept his promise.

James shook his head, not wanting to let in the same thoughts Gwen had in her head. He couldn't make the same mistakes she had. They needed to do this. They had no choice.

"Well then, Seth, where to now?" Gwen asked. "Since I know nothing of your plan."

"What we always do, my dear Gwen." Seth smiled as they hailed a cab. "We take over the city."

CHAPTER SIXTEEN

They were here.

Erik took Collin, and they headed inside Vatican City. Erik's heart raced as they crossed the barrier of salt. Inside, the demons couldn't do anything to them no matter how hard they tried. They could burn them out, of course, but Erik could just fly up in the sky and wait if he really wanted to. He didn't, though. He just wanted a few moments before the real fight began.

Collin appeared as white as a ghost. Erik wasn't sure if it was because Gwen was now in the city or if it was because this would be the end. There were no words to comfort him or make this easier, so Erik didn't say anything. He was also caught up in his own thoughts and had to focus to make this work.

They went straight to the cardinal who was in charge of the candles. He had to let them know to gather their people and be ready for the worst. There were tunnels that they could take out of the room if need be, but Erik hoped it wouldn't come to that. He wasn't going to wait until the demons began starting fires. No, he would start evacuation long before that.

The cardinal was waiting outside the room as he did every day. Erik bowed to the cardinal.

"Cardinal Jonathan. It is time."

Jonathan nodded quickly. "All right. My time has come. Come with me. We will give the information to the rest of the cardinals so they can evacuate the building if need be."

Erik noted that Jonathan's arms and legs were shaking as he led them down the hallway. He couldn't blame him—this was a lot to take in, and each cardinal didn't know what they would actually have to prepare for. But Jonathan had been around for the past two decades, and he had watched the past few Gargoyles pass. He more than likely knew this would happen on his watch.

They came across a large meeting room. Jonathan turned to the two of them. "Wait here while I summon the others."

Jonathan left Erik and Collin in the room as he wandered off. Erik let out a breath. "Are you ready, Collin?"

Collin shook his head. "No. I am not. But would anyone be ready for this?"

Erik let out a brief laugh. "No. I suppose not. Not even I feel ready for this."

Collin turned to him. "Do you think you can do it? That we can do it?"

Erik watched him for a moment. He didn't know what to say because he didn't—he didn't believe there was a possibility that they would win. Elizabeth wasn't here, and she was the cleverest. It was supposed to be her who survived, not him. But that wasn't what happened, and Erik needed to accept that. He couldn't think about what-ifs and how the past should have been different but focus on what was to come and how he would win.

He placed his hand on Collin's shoulder. "I think God

has a plan no matter what happens."

Collin rolled his eyes. "You sound like my local pastor growing up. But I know you mean it in every sense of the word. Good always prevails, right?"

Was that true? He wasn't sure, but he wanted to believe it. It seemed like good was prevalent in the beginning, but then Lucifer became corrupt and took others with him. That was when darkness began, and ever since then, it had always been a battle.

So was there good in the beginning or was Lucifer always corrupt? These were questions that ran through his mind more often than not. It was hard to think back so long ago. Had he been blind to the building temptation within his fellow comrades?

"Yeah, I suppose it does."

A few minutes passed, and the room filled with over a hundred different people who lived nearby or worked within the Vatican besides the pope. They were, of course, mainly all elderly gentlemen. Erik didn't quite agree with the fact that this religion seemed to be mainly run by old men who didn't understand how the world had changed, not to mention how the majority of the world thought and functioned, but that was for another day and not his problem. He let humans deal with human matters. But he couldn't let them all die because of a battle he brought to their doorstep.

Cardinal Jonathan nodded to him to begin. Collin was already hidden away from all the cardinals, more than likely intimidated by so many people who had power of some sort, even though Collin could easily take over this place if he really wanted to. Luckily for Erik, he didn't.

Erik stepped in the middle of the stage. "I have come to you all to warn you that demons are coming to Rome. They have made it here and will begin their descent on Vatican City. The place is surrounded by a salt barrier, but that doesn't mean they won't try to burn the place to the ground."

Murmurs began to flood the chamber. Erik waited for them to quiet down.

"I urge you to leave this location and let the battle commence. This is the best place for me to be able to take down the demons as I can weave in and out of the salt barrier, but it may cost this land."

Their voices were louder this time. Erik never understood how possessions and places could be so sacred to humans when there were more important things, especially when it came to religion. No one needed such grand areas to worship God, nor did they need relics. They only needed themselves and their connection to the divine.

"Gather what you need and leave as soon as possible. This isn't a drill or practice. It will only be a matter of time before they show up."

One of the cardinals stood up. "How do we know you are the real deal? How do we know that Cardinal Jonathan isn't lying to us about who you are?"

Erik wanted to argue with him about faith, but this wasn't the time. Erik let his wings appear and stretch out, taking up most of the area around him. All the cardinals gasped, and some even jumped up and backed away. Erik smiled a little. They gave their life to God, but seeing an Angel was still unbelievable to them.

"Now leave," Erik ordered. "Before they come."

After giving them the proof that they wanted, the members of the church vacated the room to head out of town. Erik took a deep breath in and out. One matter was settled, and now he just had to wait to see what the demons' plan was. He turned to Collin.

"Let's go up top and wait. I'm sure they will be knocking on our doors soon enough."

With that, they ventured back through the tunnels and

to the outdoors. The sun was beginning to set on the horizon, and Erik knew that it was going to be a very long night.

CHAPTER SEVENTEEN

Gwen licked the last bit of blood off her lips. She had once turned an entire theater worth of people during a Shakespeare play, but this was many more. Sure, they weren't turning the entire city, but she felt like they were getting there.

Good thing demons never actually got full and could take in as much blood as they wanted. Hell, they even used to bathe in it when they could. She missed those days. It was harder to do that now with all the forensics and constantly being monitored, although they got away with a lot due to their control over government officials.

But Rome wasn't one of those governments that they controlled, mainly due to the fact that the church was headquartered there. There were enemies no matter where they looked, and just walking through the city made her entire body hurt.

They would push through that, however. They would bring Erik out of the Vatican and battle to the end.

Would she have to give the final blow? Gwen hoped not as she didn't know if she could end someone who trusted her, even if he was using her to turn Collin. Then there was the matter of Collin.

She definitely couldn't fulfill her promise to kill him and give his head to James on a silver platter. The human had accepted Gwen—had believed her when she said she was going to turn herself in and wanted to be redeemed, even after everything. She remembered the look on his face when he realized she had used him. It had broken her heart.

Gwen turned her attention on James, who had bit another human to turn them. She needed to focus on James and how she was doing all this for him. It was their love that moved her forward, not Collin's.

He stepped forward to her and brushed his finger

against her lips. "What are you thinking about, my love?"

She smiled. "How you always did look good in red."

"Oh, is that so? Well, just wait as we will paint this entire city red before going after the last Gargoyles."

Gwen gave him a kiss. "I hope so. I wouldn't have it any other way."

James had his attention outside the café. "The others should be taking over the local law enforcement. Then we should be in the clear if anyone reports us. Are you ready to hit the next business?"

She nodded. "Always. But I have to wonder if all these minions will make a difference."

"I think they will definitely slow Erik down."

"He could just fly over them. Are we wasting our efforts? Maybe we should just burn him out."

James laughed. "You always did like to play with fire. Well, the problem with that is, as you said, he can fly, but also if we aren't careful, we can burn as well. Don't you remember when London burned down?"

She did, and they had lost a demon that day. "Fine. We will just get to making minions."

"But if you make one to send to them, Gwen, they will end you."

Gwen eyed her lover. "I haven't betrayed you."

"Again. You haven't betrayed me. Again."

He had a point there. She shrugged with her arms. "Whatever. That was so last year. This year will be different. Can't you feel it?"

"Well, I mean, we will be defeating Erik and have control over the world, so yes?" James raised an eyebrow as if she were losing it.

"It doesn't feel like it is just that. It feels like there is something else waiting for us." Gwen sighed.

"You mean like Collin?"

She shook her head. "I don't know."

"Do you sense him here?"

She took a deep breath. "He's definitely here, but he's beyond the salt barrier. I sensed him when we were getting close. They must have stayed outside the Vatican to make sure Collin could sense us."

"Well then, I guess his survival helped us a little for making sure this was indeed where Erik was."

Gwen folded her arms in front of herself. "Are you trying to pick a fight, James?"

"No, not at all, my love. I just can't wait to tear him apart limb from limb."

Her heart sank. She knew that wasn't an empty

threat. She didn't want to watch him kill Collin again. She wanted Collin to finish out his life like he originally intended. Then she screwed it up because she started to feel attached and James got jealous.

But she couldn't change the past, and she had to keep moving forward to the future that she and James fought so hard for.

The bodies began to stir as demons possessed the new minions. Gwen peered down at them. "Well, shall we give them their orders?"

James nodded. "Yes, let's."

They spent most of the night transforming humans into minions and sending them to the barrier. They had enough now to surround the entire area. Collin and Erik would have to defeat them in order to get past. Now they needed to finish up and draw them out.

The four of them gathered together just east of the Vatican. They could see Collin and Erik in the distance, watching them as they prepared. They knew the battle was about to commence, but they hadn't moved a muscle. Perhaps they were waiting or stalling to make sure everyone left the area. They cared more about humans than their own life. It was pathetic.

Gwen folded her arms in front of herself. "Well then, what's the next part of the plan? Sorry to burst your bubble, but I kind of need to know at this point."

Seth eyed her. "I don't know. Can you be trusted?"

She couldn't believe what she was hearing. Yes, she had her doubts, but this was ridiculous. "We are in front of the Vatican. What the hell do you think I would be able to do?"

"You're a clever girl, Gwen. I'm sure you would figure out some way to fuck this up," Jürgen commented.

She turned to James. "So, what do I need to do?"

"We need to convince a human to go in there and plead with Erik and Collin to come out of there. Maybe threaten a family or something?"

That made sense since no minion could go through the barrier. A human, however, could.

Gwen peered around but only found minions thus far. She used her superspeed to move farther through the city and found a couple who were walking together. What sort of crazy couple walked so early in the morning? Ones that were about to die, that's who.

Her eyes turned yellow, and her fangs grew as she grabbed the woman. Both of them screamed as Gwen gave her demands. "Go into Vatican City and tell the two men that they must leave or else your girlfriend dies. Do you understand?"

Gwen slowly brought her teeth to the girl's throat. She wasn't going to actually bite as that would make minions. At least, not yet.

"Fine! Fine! I will do it!" The man stumbled as he made a run for it toward Erik and Collin.

Gwen grinned as she watched. "Let the battle begin."

CHAPTER EIGHTEEN

Collin could sense the four demons surrounding Vatican City. Not only that, but there were enough minions that they couldn't cross the border without being clawed. He would have to be careful as the minions might not be smart, but they could scratch and bite. They were like feral dogs or cats wanting to destroy anything they could get their hands on.

The goal was to keep them off Erik's back as Erik tried to take down each demon individually. Collin wondered how long he would be able to hold them off, if much at all. He knew he would be safe going back across the salt barrier, and the goal was to stay as close as they could to it, but the demons would try their hardest to get them far away.

It was going to be a very interesting battle to say the least.

In front of him, beyond the barrier, Gwen appeared with a human in her hands. The woman was crying as Gwen had a tight grip on her hair. As Collin was trying to figure out what she was going to do, a man came running toward them.

"Please help! My girlfriend! Some demon has her! She ordered me to get you. I don't know what to do!" The man was sobbing and barely getting the words out.

So since they couldn't get minions past the barrier, they sent in regular humans using threats. Collin glanced at Gwen who was smiling with fangs brushing against the neck of the women she held. This was how it was going to be—they weren't going to play fair. They never did.

Collin had to remember to stick to the plan as they couldn't mess up or all this was going to be for nothing. A couple of humans couldn't deter them from how they were going to fight. Their sacrifices would be worth it.

At least, that was what Collin kept telling himself.

"Please! Help her!" The man was on his knees now, peering up at the two of them. Erik took a deep breath in as he glanced up at Gwen and then the dawning sky.

"It is time."

Collin knew what he meant by that. Their fight would begin. Collin pulled out one of his water guns as Erik pulled out a rapier. Collin also had a rapier, but he wouldn't use it until completely necessary. Using the holy water guns was a lot easier.

"Stay here. I will get your girlfriend back. And you can't leave the Vatican City. Do you hear me? Or else you might be attacked," Erik explained as he started forward.

The man didn't seem to understand, but he didn't move as Collin followed Erik. Erik stepped up to the edge to face Gwen.

"Let the woman go," Erik ordered.

Gwen grinned. "Aw, come on Erik, I will only take a nibble. Then she can join all these minions that want to tear off your flesh."

"You have already killed plenty of humans tonight. Do you really need to kill another?"

She bit her lip. "I mean, no. But it is just so much

fun. Look at her. Her life would be much happier if she were turned."

"You mean dead? The human soul doesn't stay if you bite her, Gwen. Let her go to her boyfriend."

Her eyes flickered to Collin, and Collin felt a pit in his stomach. He didn't want to see this Gwen—he wanted to see the one who used to stay up with him staring at the skies or talking about the world early in the morning while drinking whiskey. This wasn't the girl he used to know—he needed to remember that.

"I don't know—I've gotten a lot of slack for not killing who I was supposed to kill over these past couple of months. I don't want to be scolded again." Her eyes didn't leave Collin. He gulped, understanding what she meant by that.

"If you let her go, I will step outside the barrier. How does that sound?"

Her eyes widened in delight. "And bring on the end of this world? Do you think you are really ready for that?"

"I think you demons are cocky and don't know what you have coming."

She laughed, her voice sounding almost sadistic. "I have everything to lose if I lose this battle, Erik. Do you really think I would let my defenses down? Although I have to say I didn't come prepared with a sword..." She pouted a little. "And it has been oh so long since I used one."

"Well, I'm sorry you weren't prepared enough. I guess I will make it up to you and end you quickly."

"Then your precious hybrid will be dead, and you will have no one to cover your back. You wouldn't want that, now would you?"

It was rare for Collin to see Erik come a little unhinged. It all unleashed at once, shocking even Collin.

"You know what, Guinevere? I am going to have fun ending you! You know that? After all these years, after every time you tied me up and drained me of my blood, I will relish in your death."

Her grin got even wider. "So this will be the fight I have been waiting for all these years. You should have killed me when you had the chance, Erik. I won't hold back this time."

"Then let the girl go," Erik growled.

She moved her head to the side, as if debating. "Nah."

With that, she bit into the woman's throat and ripped

it out so that she wouldn't come back as a minion. Blood splashed them, and the sweet scent made Collin feel his eyes turn yellow and his fangs lengthen. He wanted more blood even though he had fed on Erik earlier. He took deep breaths to calm himself down.

The man behind them screamed as he watched his girlfriend be killed. Collin's gut felt as if it were being stabbed as the man ran toward where the body of his girlfriend lay. He reached for her but didn't have time as Gwen grabbed him and bit into his neck.

Erik glared at her. Collin watched in horror as the man's body dropped to the ground. Gwen licked her lips.

"Well then, Erik. Your move."

He reached out of the barrier for her neck, but she jumped back, laughing.

"Nice try, Erik, but you have to move a bit faster than that!"

Collin followed after Erik as he ran toward Gwen. He used the water gun to take down a few of the minions. Their once-human form was gone and now left a grotesque human shell possessed by a demon. It almost appeared as if the demons were just wearing the human skin as the minion's eyes were yellow, their nails long, their faces almost like they were transforming into werewolves.

He shot one after another as Gwen made Erik follow her into the city. Where was she taking him? Why was Erik venturing so far from the salt line? Collin didn't have the opportunity to ask but stayed near Erik, keeping the minions off his back.

Erik slashed at Gwen as she kept hopping back, laughing like it was some kind of game. The other three demons were still at their posts on the other side of the Vatican. They should have noticed Gwen moving, so why weren't they closing in yet?

That is unless they were doing what they did last time and had used blood as a decoy. Collin still would have sensed something, however, as they would have had to mask themselves with some kind of blood. So it had to be something else.

Perhaps they were tiring Erik out first with Gwen. Or perhaps there was going to be some explosion or something.

Collin kept thinking about the different possibilities, but as he kept thinking, he realized he wasn't completely paying attention to Gwen. Suddenly she appeared in front of him.

"I'm going to need to borrow this." She grabbed the hilt of his rapier and pulled it out of the sheath.

Collin gasped as he jumped back. Gwen had a smirk as she countered Erik's sword attack. Collin pointed the gun at her and shot the water. She tried to leap out of the way as Erik swung the sword, but she wasn't able to do both. The water hit her skin and burned her flesh.

"Ouch! That tingles!" She tried to smile, but Collin could see the pain in her face.

Erik swung again and again, and Gwen blocked each and every attack. She was still moving backward, drawing him away from the Vatican. Collin kept his senses alert and used the guns against the minions that reached for Erik, but they were weak and slower than Collin.

Then Erik got a swing in and went straight through Gwen's stomach. The smell of her blood filled Collin's senses, and he could barely focus. All he wanted was her blood at that moment, filling him up and making him feel whole. He shook the feeling away, trying to focus on everything else.

"Wow, Erik. Didn't think you had it in you!" She said as she jumped back. She touched her wound and licked her lips as Erik charged at her.

"Erik," Collin called out. "We've got to move back! Before—"

And that was when he sensed it—the other demons were moving in.

CHAPTER NINETEEN

James could sense Gwen's blood.

She was very good at annoying anyone she came across, even the Gargoyles. Especially the Gargoyles, if James were honest. They wanted her dead the most and yet were never successful at it.

That was their cue, however, to circle in on Erik. Since they couldn't sense him that well, they made Gwen draw him out until he was far enough that they could surround him and block his way back to the Vatican. Gwen would let herself get injured so the smell of blood was the indication she was ready.

It was all going according to plan so far. That was if Gwen wasn't tricking them at that moment.

It saddened James that the thought crossed his mind and was unfortunately a possible one. James was the closest one to Gwen and would appear to her first, so if she was crossing them, at least he could punish her first.

As he rounded the corner, he felt something burn his face. James hissed as he realized he had just gotten shot in the face with holy water. His eyes were burning as he backed up, not sure what the stupid hybrid was going to do next. He couldn't see Collin, but he knew it was him. He was the stupid human who thought up holy water guns.

The problem was Collin could strike while he couldn't see. James couldn't sense him, mainly because Collin thought of washing himself with salt water constantly. It dulled the demon's scent, and James couldn't pinpoint the hybrid. James kept jumping back, heading toward Jürgen, trusting that the demon would protect him if need be. Slowly his eyes began to heal, and just as he could make out a blurry vision of Collin coming at him with a knife, James grabbed his wrist and punched him square in the jaw. Collin flew back and into a wall of a building, making the brick crumble around him. He coughed up blood. Served him right.

James's eyes were still healing, but he didn't let it hold him back. He was able to make out most shapes. Everything would just be a little bit fuzzy.

"Oh, you picked the wrong demon to mess with today," James growled as he stepped up to Collin. "I am going to have fun killing you again."

Collin stood up and pulled out a knife. "No, this is going to be the end for all you demons. And I look forward to finally seeing your kind destroyed."

The kid had spunk. If James didn't hate him so much, perhaps Collin would have been a good asset. But it was too late for that. James used his powers to move forward quickly. Collin swung his knife around, trying to deter James. It only made James laugh.

"You really think you can hurt me with that puny knife?"

Part of the knife cut into James's skin, which shouldn't have hurt much, but the moment the blade made contact it stung. James yelped out in pain and grabbed the wound. It wasn't healing—at least not quickly.

"Silver dipped in holy water. What do you think?"

Collin smiled.

"I think I am going to end you quickly instead of drawing it out like I was going to!" James jumped forward, swiping at Collin's arm, but Collin was quicker. He slashed James again, making him let out a hiss.

"What do you think you are doing?" A voice growled behind him. He turned to find Jürgen there. "We need to surround Erik if this is going to work!"

James glared at him. "This hybrid is only going to cause trouble. We need to take him down first if we want to take down Erik. Otherwise he's going to attack us when our backs are turned."

"You know as well as I that isn't what the plan is! Leave him alone until we are done dealing with Erik!"

James turned back to Collin and scowled. Jürgen was right. They needed everyone on Erik in order to take the Gargoyles out. Collin was just a distraction.

But he wanted him dead more than anything. He was the reason Gwen couldn't shake off the feeling of redemption—he was the reason she felt more human.

Of course he blamed Gwen for her deceit as well, and Collin wasn't completely responsible, but that didn't mean he didn't want him dead any less. This hybrid thought Gwen was his, and James did not like to share. Flirting to feed was something completely different than what Gwen had done to Collin and how she'd brought him in.

"Fine." James turned back to Jürgen as they hurried toward Gwen, who James could sense was still bleeding. He then realized he had left Gwen to fight on her own against a Gargoyles. Erik could have taken her out as she was already wounded. Collin had distracted James from his true objective—get out of this alive with Gwen.

Collin was following after them, and although he was faster than a Gargoyles, he wasn't as fast as a demon. James wasn't sure if that was because he didn't feed as much as they did or if hybrids were always a little slower. It had been a long time since he had dealt with one.

They rounded the corner to find Erik had Gwen up against a wall. Her eyes were wide as Erik started to swing down his rapier at her.

James grabbed the rapier that he assumed Gwen had dropped and rushed toward Erik. Since Erik had his back turned to him, he assumed that the Gargoyles wouldn't know he was coming. Unfortunately, that wasn't the case. Erik must have seen Gwen peer behind him as he rotated his momentum and blocked James's attack.

"And here I thought I would finally end that bitch of yours," Erik snarled.

This caught James by surprise, as Erik always kept a cool head. Erik must have realized he couldn't hold back any longer. This made James smile.

"I see she got to you. She always has a way of doing that, doesn't she?"

Erik screamed out as he swung again and again at James. The angrier that Erik became, the more James laughed. Jürgen attacked from Erik's side, but Erik was able to push James back and swing at Jürgen, causing Jürgen to jump back.

James tried to sense Seth but couldn't focus long enough to be able to tell. James threw Jürgen the sword. "Cover me while I tend to Gwen."

Jürgen grunted but knew that they needed her. Quickly, James knelt down to her. "Don't worry, your Prince Charming is here."

Gwen smiled but coughed up a little blood. "Damn, those swords hurt. He's still got some fight in him for being an old guy."

She still had her humor, which was a good sign. He picked her up and used speed to find themselves a minion. It seemed that Collin had done a good job of taking out most of them in the surrounding area. Stupid hybrid—this was why he thought it would be better to take him out first, but Seth was in charge, not him.

They found a group of humans hiding in a café. The door was locked, but James simply kicked it down. Gwen didn't hesitate to grab one of them and bite into their neck. James grabbed the two others and held them, waiting for Gwen to finish hers and move on to the next.

She did just that, and James bit into the last human in the café. With the energy, he was able to heal up the last wounds that Collin had given him. He dropped the human on the floor and wiped the blood off his face.

"Well then, sweetie, shall we get back to it?"

Gwen nodded. "Yes, let's."

CHAPTER TWENTY

Erik wished he could tear these demons limb from limb and relish in their deaths. He knew it was wrong—he knew he was thinking like a demon and needed to stop, but after everything, he just wanted to see them dead.

Why was it that they were winning? Why was it that he was completely outnumbered? Was it because they had no guilt in killing? Was it because they would do whatever it took?

Well, they were in for a surprise, Erik thought. He was going to do whatever it took as well.

He tried to save the two humans that Gwen was using to get to him. He knew he should have let it go, as two human lives were nothing compared to what was at stake, but he wasn't backing down to begin with. He was ready to fight, but Gwen still killed them both with a sadistic smile on her face.

It was the last straw—he was done playing her games.

Erik struck at Jürgen again and again. It was apparent that swordsmanship was Jürgen's strong suit. This surprised Erik a little as the large man didn't seem like he would be into swords as much as he would be into hand-to-hand combat and guns. Gwen was the one who liked swords. At least that was what it had seemed like over the centuries.

He almost had her too. If James hadn't shown up when he did, he would have taken her life. However, that would have meant he would have taken Collin's life. It was a price to pay as Gwen was the one he needed to look out for the most.

And she was the one he wanted to kill most.

"Someone seems to have fixated on something else." Jürgen grinned. "What did Gwen do to bring you out of your hidey-hole?"

Erik swung the sword harder, which made Jürgen jump back a little bit, surprises he had so much power in him still.

"Damn, even mentioning her name makes you more furious. Have to hand it to her. She knows how to piss people off."

"You all would know that since she has betrayed the demons too. She's only fighting for herself. How do you know she isn't going to mess it all up again just for fun?"

Jürgen laughed. "That's simple. Because I promised to kill her if she does."

"You know as well as I she doesn't die easily. There's always someone who shows up to save her, whether it be James or Collin."

"That's true. But I doubt that hybrid of yours is going to save her again."

Erik wasn't too sure of that. Gwen could be quite compelling. That was her problem and why she was such a menace. It was why Erik wanted her dead.

Suddenly Erik watched as Jürgen screamed out in pain and whipped his head around. Erik noticed Collin behind him, shooting Jürgen with the holy water gun. Erik had to hand it to Collin. He came up with the best ideas.

As Jürgen had his back turned, Erik stabbed through his ribs. Unfortunately, he missed Jürgen's heart.

Jürgen let out a scream as he leaped out of reach of the rapier, blood now covering the sword and soaking his shirt. Jürgen hissed as he glared at Erik.

"You will pay for that!" Jürgen yelled and then murmured, "Where the hell is Seth?"

Erik didn't like the fact that he hadn't come across the fourth demon. What was he up to? Where was he going?

But now with Jürgen barely being able to stand and most of the minions still a ways away due to Collin destroying the ones around him, this was his chance. He didn't know when Gwen and James would be back. He couldn't hesitate.

Erik moved forward after Jürgen. With the wound, Jürgen could run back fast enough and was barely able to keep up his sword.

"Damn it," Jürgen said through gritted teeth. "Where are they?"

Erik wasn't even going to answer as he swung toward the demon's throat to decapitate him when suddenly there were loud repetitive sounds and Erik felt pain through his entire back. He yelled out in pain.

Spinning around, he found Seth with an automatic rifle. If Erik cursed, he would have done so right then and there.

There was only one thing he could do, and it was fly up. He didn't want to do that as he didn't want to leave Collin there by himself. Erik knew he would have to try to grab him, but Jürgen was between them.

Erik did a slight hop to leap over the injured demon and grabbed Collin. Seth didn't seem to care that Jürgen was in the line of fire and kept shooting. Six more hit into Erik, but he didn't hesitate as he wrapped one arm around Collin and flew up in the air.

It was just in time too as James and Gwen appeared, now back at full strength. Erik hurried toward the Vatican so he could catch a breath before going out and fighting. Seth shot in the air at them, but he was able to escape those bullets.

Erik dropped Collin down on the pavement as he himself collapsed within the boundary of the salt. Blood had soaked his clothes now, and although he could heal quite fast without blood like the demons, it would still take some time.

But did he have time? The demons would be able to

get blood and heal their wounds and be at one hundred percent.

It wasn't fair, Erik thought. They had the advantage in most aspects of this fight.

He glanced at Collin, who seemed in pretty good shape. At least he had that going for him. Collin stepped over to Erik.

"You need to stay closer to here. They almost had you circled."

Erik shook his head. "I always have the ability to fly up."

"But what if they stab you in the wings? You will have to wait to heal."

He had a point there. "Fine, I will stay around here. My anger got the better of me. It's rare for it to do that."

Erik took a deep breath and let it out slowly. He needed to focus. He would have to try to draw out one demon out at a time, which he was almost successful in doing except one would always show up right at the last moment to save them.

He could always grab one and take them up in the air, but the problem was that then they would be in close quarters, and that was never a good idea—not when they had sharp teeth and claws. Erik turned his attention to the salt barrier. What would happen if he tried to forcibly bring them through? Would it be like dragging them through a wall?

At least it seemed that a good chunk of the minions had been taken out by Collin, but there were still many more. While he had the time, Collin went over to where he was storing more water guns that were filled. At least here he wouldn't run out, as long as he was able to get back within the salt barrier.

"Are you ready?" Erik asked as he could see the demons heading in their direction.

Collin nodded. "As much as I will ever be."

CHAPTER TWENTY-ONE

Gwen was so over this. She just wanted to kill the Gargoyles and it all be over with. But no, Erik had to go and snap and use his anger to fight. It was much easier to fight with anger and everything to lose—it meant one wouldn't hold back.

Which is what exactly happened. Gwen would have lost her head if James hadn't shown up and taken her away to heal. He was always there when she needed him, and she just hoped that she would be there when he needed her.

They had made their way back to where the last Gargoyles awaited. He was weakened by Seth's attack. Gwen was a bit mad that he hadn't given them all guns as they would have come in handy earlier. But there was something to be said about using one's hands to take down a Gargoyles. It was like the olden days when they didn't use weapons at all, way back when. Gwen missed those days and felt that guns were barbaric, but they were efficient.

Gwen had picked up the sword that Jürgen had dropped. She did fancy a sword, however, as nothing beat the sound of metal clashing, and one slipup could lead to one's head chopped off. It was thrilling.

Erik was within view now, and Gwen wondered if she would have to go through the whole ordeal again to coax him out. For some reason she doubted it as Erik had the look of intent on his face. He had calmed down, which made Gwen sad. She liked him when he was angry.

Collin was next to him—his water guns reloaded. She hated those things, although she had to give him props as they were a clever device. She was glad no one had thought about it earlier, but water guns were a rather new invention in terms of their lives. The

Gargoyles probably didn't even know they existed.

Another smart idea would have been salt hula-hoops, but she wasn't going to be giving them the idea.

"Well, what's your next move, Erik?" Gwen called out playfully. "Or have you given up and we will have to burn you out?"

Seth growled. "We aren't burning him out. Fire can kill us too."

She rolled her eyes. "I know that, but it doesn't mean we can't threaten it, does it?"

"Unless he wants to call us on our bluff and decide to wait until we do it."

He had a point there. Erik wouldn't be one to start a fire, but he might want one to use against them. But Erik knew that he could be killed in the fire as well, so she doubted it.

"We could always make a truce for the next hundred years." Erik grinned. "Leave each other alone and you could do whatever you wanted without worry. Unlike Lucifer, I actually keep my promises."

Gwen actually liked that idea but knew that in a century, Lucifer could come and punish them. She didn't look forward to that part of the deal. Besides, right when the deal was over, Erik would have come up with a plan to destroy them all.

That is if there weren't other surprises waiting for them when Erik died.

Erik closed his eyes for a moment, as if in meditation. Seth raised his gun. Gwen wasn't sure how many more bullets he had, but just as he was about to fire, Erik leaped high up in the air, using his wings to fly.

It just wasn't fair—why couldn't they still use their wings? Gwen supposed it was because they had been ripped out of their backs and they had been chained down to Earth. It was like they weren't welcome back into Heaven or something.

Erik had his sword ready and came flying down at the four of them. The other three demons jumped out of the way as Gwen swung her sword to block him. The force pushed her back, and she hit the ground.

She realized she should have jumped out of the way.

Collin stayed within the salt circle and shot out at the minions that were gathering and coming toward them. Gwen hissed and reached for him, but her hand smacked on the barrier. Wretched thing. She hated salt more than anything—especially since now it was practically in all food.

"You know what I have always wondered?" Erik asked from behind her.

She realized she had let her guard down when she tried to grab Collin. Before she could spin around, Erik kicked her hand into the barrier. If he had simply kicked without her being there, he would have gone through it. But since she was there, her hand hit it like a wall. She felt her bones crack, and she yelped as she dropped her sword.

"I've always wondered how high the barrier goes for you lot. Shall we find out?"

Gwen tried to jump away, but she was too late. Erik had grabbed her by the back of the neck and was pushing her straight into the barrier while lifting her up.

Gwen had been tortured in many different ways between the demons punishing her for something she did and the Gargoyles fighting her. Usually the worst was when they took her up high and she felt the chains to Earth pulling her down, but that wasn't much worse than a plane ride.

But having one's face shoved into a salt barrier as she was dragged up was much, much worse.

It was similar to the holy water in that it was burning and eroding the flesh on her face. She could hardly see anything but simply felt as if her skin was being ripped away.

So a Gargoyles could be sadistic if pushed far enough.

There were shots being fired around them. At least Seth was trying to save her. Perhaps he was just using the chance to take down Erik. It was probably the latter as Seth didn't really care if she died or not.

A few of the bullets hit Erik, and Gwen felt Erik turn as he faced his attacker. She took the opportunity to twist in his hand and kicked him away. Erik let go of her.

She still couldn't see. She realized that now as she tried to peer down and see how much it was going to hurt when she hit the ground.

"Son of a—"

Gwen landed on something soft and then felt flesh against her mouth.

"Bite, Gwen." It was James. She did just that, James's blood filling her being. She felt her face heal and let go of his arm. She didn't want to take too much and weaken him, but she needed to take enough to survive.

"That hurt," Gwen stated. "I don't recommend letting

him do that to you."

"Yeah, that looked like an experience I wouldn't want to try."

"I'm not sure how to take him down, James. I thought this was going to be much easier. Seems he has a lot more fight in him than I could imagine."

"It doesn't help that Collin is staying inside and just shooting us with that stupid water." James growled as he looked at Collin.

This was probably their original plan. Gwen grinned, realizing she was able to get Erik to come out far away because of what she did. Perhaps she could piss Erik off again. But what could she do? He probably wasn't going to fall for her shenanigans once more.

Gwen bit her lip as she glanced around. Seth was giving him a run for his money with his guns. Gwen was surprised Jürgen didn't have any, but it appeared that he had picked up Gwen's sword. In all the years Gwen had known Jürgen, a sword seemed to have been his favorite. He studied more hours than she had under all the masters he could. He liked the feeling of slicing into skin, no matter what the weapon was. That was why he would pin enemies outside his castle and drank their blood as Vlad Dracul.

"Remind me not to piss off Jürgen."

James laughed. "I think you are way past that. He hates your guts."

She grinned. That was for sure. But that didn't solve how they were going to get Erik away from the salt barrier so that Collin would come out of his hiding place.

"You don't think that Seth brought some grenades with him, do you?" Gwen asked.

"No fires or explosions, remember?"

She sighed. Then a thought occurred to her. "Wait here. I will be right back."

And with that, Gwen left the fight.

CHAPTER TWENTY-TWO

Collin didn't like the fact that Gwen had disappeared. He knew he would be safe inside the barrier, but that didn't mean she couldn't cause trouble.

It would be stupid for him to follow her and try to stop whatever she was doing as he needed to help Erik with the other three. Now that James wasn't preoccupied with Gwen, he joined the other two in trying to get to Erik.

Not if he could help it. Collin shot at James. He snarled as he glared at Collin. Collin was really glad the demon couldn't get to him. Collin had a feeling the moment he stepped beyond the barrier James was going to do his best to try to kill him. That was apparent when they ran into each other earlier.

He turned his attention to Jürgen and tried to aim, but Jürgen was just out of reach. If only he could get closer without exposing himself. But if Erik fought any farther away, he might have to step outside the barrier.

And that would be when James killed him.

Although James was trying to ready himself to attack Erik, it was apparent he was keeping an eye on Collin to see when he would step outside the barrier. Collin gulped and mentally told himself he would have to keep his guns full if he wanted to survive. He had a knife, which was nice for close combat, but he wished he hadn't lost his sword so early in the fight. When they battled minions in London, he wasn't so quick to lose his sword. Gwen was a lot stronger than those minions, however, so he shouldn't have been surprised. He should have been on his guard more, but that was the past, and he needed to focus on the battle at hand.

It seemed that Seth was running out of bullets. He tossed his gun aside and pulled out a long sword. Collin wondered why the others didn't seem to be armed like he was. He didn't understand demon logic, so he was just going to let it go. It probably had to do with the fact that they didn't trust each other, most importantly Gwen and probably James. They didn't seem to play by the rules ever.

He still hadn't caught sight of Gwen. He focused a bit on her scent and noticed that she was all the way out past the Colosseum. What could she be doing? Collin wondered. Was she making more minions?

She seemed to be too far for minions. There was something else she was looking for. For all Collin knew, she had stashed away something a long time ago and was retrieving it. He didn't like where his mind was going and decided to focus on the three demons in front of him.

Collin shot out at Seth and James, both of whom hissed at him as the water hit their skin. Jürgen was still too far as he slashed at Erik, who was doing a good job blocking both his and Seth's attacks. It reminded Collin of *Star Wars: The Phantom Menace* when Qui-Gon Jinn and Obi-Wan were battling Darth Maul, except in this case it was the opposite. Erik was the good guy and not the Sith.

James jumped into the fight, careful of the sword as

he tried to punch Erik and scratch him with his nails. Collin shot more of the water at him, but they had quickly gone out of reach.

"Screw this. I have to help."

Collin crossed the barrier, and just as he did, James turned his full attention on Collin. Collin wondered if he should turn right back around and go inside the barrier, but that wouldn't solve anything. He had to put up a fight or else this would be the end of everything.

"Oh, I have been waiting to do this for a long time." James's eyes flashed yellow as he used his speed to appear behind Collin. Now he couldn't run back inside the barrier.

Collin was careful to turn in a way that didn't leave his back to the other two demons. He shot at him with his water gun. James moved before the water touched him.

"You aren't going to get me that easy."

James's voice felt as if it were surrounding him as James quickly circled him. If it weren't for the fact that Collin also had superspeed, he wouldn't have been able to keep up with James. Thank goodness he could.

He aimed where James should be, but that didn't seem to work as James jumped back and forth. Collin knew he couldn't stop shooting or else the demon would get closer, but if he kept at it, he would run out of water.

Just like what James was hoping.

Changing tactics, Collin pulled out the knife and jumped forward at James. He would just have to hope he had enough of a fight in him to battle James until Erik could take down the two demons. So far he seemed to be holding his own against the two. Erik was a good swordsman, and Collin doubted that he would have any problems while he kept James distracted. All he had to worry about was Gwen, wherever she was.

Then Collin had a good idea.

"So, where did Gwen go?" Collin asked, hoping the mention of her would distract James a bit. When Gwen disappeared, confusion flooded James's face. Collin doubted he knew what she was up to.

"None of your business!" James tried to grab him, but Collin stabbed the knife into his hand. James let out an agonizing scream.

"Perhaps she left so you would be done a number. Maybe she won't come back." Collin knew that wasn't the case, but if there was any doubt in James's mind, it would make him angrier and angrier.

"Shut up, you useless hybrid!" James lashed out. Collin was definitely hitting a nerve.

"Is this what she did the first time? When she left you standing there in Germany?"

Collin realized there was a point to when James would be so pissed that if he got ahold of Collin, it was going to hurt. And he did just that. James landed a punch square on Collin's jaw. Collin went flying back into the building, his body breaking the brick and concrete.

"Shit," Collin whispered. He peered down to find that he was still holding his knife. At least he had that going for him.

James was upon him in milliseconds, beating his fist down onto Collin.

"She is my girl! Don't you dare act like you know her! I have been in love with her since the beginning of time! Your pathetic human mind can't even comprehend how long ago that was! Do you understand? There is no way you can even begin to have the deep love that I have for her!"

Collin knew he should have just kept his mouth shut and tried to stab James, which was getting harder to do with each and every second.

"And yet she still saved me that night. It must kill you to know she had any sort of feeling for me."

Yup, Collin thought, this was how he was going to die. James wrapped his hand around Collin's throat, pinning him to wall. He pulled his hand back as he was about to rip Collin's heart out.

"I have goodies!" Gwen's voice came from behind him.

James hesitated. It wasn't for long, just a moment, but it was enough for Collin to use his knife and stab James in the arm. James yelped as he let go of Collin's throat. Collin used his quick speed to leap to the salt barrier and collapse onto the ground, thirst engulfing his senses as he lay down on the stone.

He needed blood or else he wasn't going to keep his sanity much longer.

CHAPTER TWENTY-THREE

James snapped his attention to Gwen. "You did that on purpose!"

Her eyes widened in surprise. Perhaps he was wrong, but James had a gut-wrenching feeling it was all an act. "But I was just excited for what I found."

Now that he wasn't dealing with Collin, he looked at what she had in her hands. She held up a couple of gladiator-style shields and both long and short swords. James perked up.

"Where did you get those?"

She grinned. "I saw an ad for a gladiator school while on the plane. I figured they would have weapons for reenactments, and I was right."

Gwen threw him one of the long swords and a short sword. She kept one of each for herself as well.

"Do you think we will need the shields?" she asked.

James shook his head. "No, not yet. I think two swords will be better, especially since there are four of us. There is no way Erik will be able to counter all our attacks."

She dropped the shields as she followed him to where the Gargoyles fought. Erik had been holding his own against Jürgen and Seth. James was surprised how much stamina he had, but he supposed if he was the last of his kind, he too would put up a pretty big fight.

"Surprise!" Gwen laughed as she jumped into the fight. Erik ducked and lifted his sword to block hers. Jürgen took the chance and stabbed Erik straight into the side. Erik let out a cry of pain.

This was happening, James thought. They were going to defeat the last Gargoyles.

Before he could be attacked again, Erik jumped up in the air. The only problem they had was that they couldn't go after him in the air and had no way of stopping him from doing that other than stabbing him where the wings met his back. That was hard to do, however, and it was probable that Erik would jump up out of the way before contact.

James saw something fly up after Erik in the air. He turned to find Gwen also had grabbed a lasso. She smiled. "I figured it would come in handy!"

Erik was yanked back and was falling to the ground for a moment. He figured out what had happened and used his sword to cut away the lasso. Gwen frowned.

"Damn, I thought that would work."

James wished it would have as well, but they didn't take into consideration that he had a sharp weapon and was also stronger than the rope in general. They watched as Erik flew back into the salt barrier. The four of them lined up and watched as he collapsed to the ground next to Collin.

Collin at this point was breathing heavily, and his eyes were staying that yellowish glow that marked him as part demon. Gwen started humming a tune as she paced back and forth.

"What are you doing, Gwen?" Seth growled. "Do not go against the plan like you and James have been doing this entire time."

James turned to him. "Someone had to deal with the hybrid that has been shooting holy water at us."

"If you two hadn't disappeared, we would have taken Erik down by now!"

James rolled his eyes. "No, we would have simply made him jump back into the barrier earlier."

Seth glared at him, but he knew he had a point. He watched as Erik checked on Collin. He wondered if he would give him blood. James doubted it as Erik had lost a lot of energy and wouldn't risk wasting any.

Gwen bit her lip. "Let me take care of him."

"No." All three of them answered.

She kept pacing. "But he's so hungry. We can use this to our advantage."

"If you do it, I will end you," Jürgen warned. "And don't think I'm lying. If you die, so does Collin so it would be a win-win for me."

James glared at Jürgen, but Jürgen didn't care. James didn't like the fact that was what Jürgen and Seth were thinking—that if they had to, they could kill Gwen to get to Collin. It didn't bode well for any trouble she might cause.

And she always caused some trouble one or another.

Gwen turned to James and smiled. She brought her finger to her mouth and bit it. The scent of her blood filled James's senses. He wanted more than anything to lick that blood off her finger before it dripped on the ground.

Which meant Collin would feel the same way.

James grabbed Gwen's wrist and licked the blood. Gwen didn't watch him but glanced back at Collin. He was trying to stand up, but Erik was pulling him back. The more time that passed, the more rabid he was becoming. Collin was yanking and trying to get out of Erik's reach when finally he succeeded.

Gwen's smile grew larger. "Yes, come here little hybrid."

Without warning, Jürgen threw a punch at Gwen. It hit her right in the nose.

"Ow! Fuck! Jürgen, what the hell?"

"We just said to leave him alone, and you tried to coax him out! Who knows what you were going to do with him! For all we know, you would have given him your blood and then sided with Erik. Just let him lie there dying, and we can take down Erik!" Jürgen shouted at her.

He had a point. Collin was struggling and wouldn't

be able to fight any longer. If Gwen played with Collin and possibly gave him blood, then he would be strong again.

The question was, was she doing it for fun or was it because she really did want to help Erik? Gwen rubbed her cheek where Jürgen had punched her.

"Fine. What are you going to do to get Erik out of there? Apparently getting Collin to come out isn't how you want to do it."

"We wait," Seth answered. "He will come out eventually. Or else we will start it on fire."

Gwen clapped her hands together. "Yay! A fire!"

James brought her close and kissed her on the lips. "You are so adorable when you want to see chaos."

She kissed him again. "Aren't I though?" She glanced back at Collin, who was still watching them. She frowned a little, which made James wonder if she did in fact want to help him instead of destroy him.

CHAPTER TWENTY-FOUR

Erik didn't know what to do.

He was tired, weak, and Collin was on the edge of breaking. If he let go of him, he would go to Gwen, and who knew what she was up to. The other demons seemed mad at her, but even if she was going to give him her blood, it didn't mean she was helping them. It could have been to get to Erik as Collin would cross the barrier.

"Think," Erik whispered to himself. "What can you do?"

There was nothing other than trying to take them down, but now that Gwen had gone and got more weapons, it was going to be impossible for Erik to fight them. Collin was able to take out many of the minions, but the demons were the real problem. Even if he wounded one, another would come.

And now Collin was weak and couldn't last much longer without blood. He had no one on his side.

He couldn't worry about Collin, as it was more important for Erik to survive, but he felt bad for the boy. He was severely wounded, and if he didn't get blood, he would be weakened to the point of breaking and possibly acting like a demon. He didn't need another demon on his hands.

The problem was Erik didn't have any more energy to give him. He didn't know what to do. Should he run —fly off somewhere with Collin? No, with how much blood they had spilled, the demons would be able to follow and find them quickly. There was nowhere to run. This fight had to end.

"Come on, Erik! Let the poor hybrid go!" Gwen taunted. Jürgen kicked her, and she fell to the ground, laughing. They were arguing still. It was apparent that Collin wasn't where their attention was or at least not what they were supposed to be focused on.

James and Gwen, it seemed, had been focusing on Collin more than Erik. Erik had a feeling. It was because of two completely different reasons, however, as Gwen wanted to keep Collin for herself and James wanted him dead.

Erik peered down at Collin. He was breathing heavily and holding himself tight now. As Erik watched him, he heard a voice in the back of his head.

"Trust him."

It sounded like Elizabeth. What did she mean? How could Erik trust him any more than he already had? Perhaps there was something he was missing—perhaps there was something that Erik could do with Collin. He bent down to Collin's level.

"If I fail, go to these coordinates. It is where the gate is and where Jesus was buried." Erik gave him the coordinates as Collin shook his head.

"I'm not going to last much longer. Just kill me so I don't break."

Erik patted his shoulder. "You aren't going to break. Now, I am going to try to weaken them a little more and come back here. When I do, you have to promise me to do exactly what I tell you. Got it?"

Collin nodded and Erik stood up and stared at the four demons. Perhaps he would take one out in this kamikaze move. Perhaps not. But there would be no going back.

Erik jumped up and flew forward straight at them. The demons readied their swords, their eyes appearing like predators lusting after their kill. Erik wasn't able to block all of them and felt as two of the swords pierced his skin. He bit his tongue, not wanting to scream out. One of them was Gwen, and she stabbed him straight in the stomach. Curse her persistence.

He would have to be careful to make sure they didn't damage his wings, as then he wouldn't be able to fly and get back to Collin. Turning back around, he went in again, slicing and hacking at the demons. If he could knock one of their swords out of their hands, then he could grab them and fly them up in the air, but having a demon in close quarters was difficult, especially when he was this weak.

Which meant he wasn't going to get anywhere with this—he was simply weakening himself until he could barely see straight.

Erik was having trouble keeping his sword level, and anytime he swung he felt as if the sword he had clashed with would go through his own sword and slice right through his neck. If that happened, he would die. He couldn't let the demons kill him.

Tumbling back through the salt barrier, he crawled back to where Collin was still struggling with his conscience. This was the only way to destroy the demons.

Erik didn't know if what he was doing would make a difference or if he was having faith in the wrong idea. What he was about to do had never been done before, and for all he knew, it was just going to cause the demons to win.

But as the voice he heard said—he had to believe in Collin.

"Collin, drink my blood," Erik ordered.

"But," Collin began.

"You promised me you would do what I ordered. Now drink it!"

Collin didn't hesitate again as he bit into Erik's neck. Erik counted to three, and then took his hand and jammed it into his own chest.

CHAPTER TWENTY-FIVE

Gwen didn't know what she had just witnessed.

Her eyes were suddenly blinded as white light came pouring out of Erik. Moments before, he had let Collin bite him and then pulled out his own heart.

Erik had killed himself. The last Gargoyles was dead.

That should have been good news, but with this light, Gwen was beginning to doubt they were in the clear. Whatever the light was, it moved up in the air. Gwen shielded her eyes from it and tried to concentrate.

Was that Collin?

Sure enough, Collin was the one in the air, and he appeared like anAngel—golden light emanated from his body in every direction.

"Well, fuck," Gwen whispered to herself. James grabbed her and started running.

"We have to get out of here!"

Gwen wasn't going to argue. Whatever that was, she wasn't going to be able to control him with her blood anymore. He wasn't some human-demon mix. No, now that boy hadAngel blood in him or was possessed by Erik. Either way, they needed to get the hell out of there.

The gate should be open. Erik was dead. She glanced up at the sky, and sure enough, it appeared darker, even with the light coming off Collin. Gwen gulped.

She was right—if they won the battle, there would just be something new that they would have to destroy.

It was clear that they didn't have to destroy Collin in order to open the gates, as there was a sort of darkness emanating around them, but she knew Erik had given him orders to go to the gate and protect it at all cost. But whatever Collin was now, there would be no way that he could take on all four of them at once, right?

James seemed to disagree as he was running as fast

as he could. Truth be told, they simply didn't know. This had never happened before. Gwen had killed a few Gargoyles herself, but nothing like this had ever happened. Perhaps it was because his soul wasn't damned.

Gwen glanced back to see what had happened to Jürgen and Seth and whether they were stupid enough to stick around to find out what power the double hybrid possessed. They were right behind them, running for their lives.

Why did their luck suck so much? Why couldn't anything ever go according to plan? Why couldn't it be easy? It had been over four thousand years since they were dropped off on this planet—and it never got better.

The light was still emanating from Collin. He didn't seem to be moving, as if he was figuring out what he was and what was going on. Gwen couldn't blame him for that, as it had taken them some time to figure everything out. She just hoped they would be out of the city before he realized what he could do.

And she prayed to Lucifer that the hybrid couldn't still use his demon senses to locate them. It seemed sacrilege to pray, even if it was to Lucifer, but she didn't know what else to do. She had never been so afraid in all her life, even when Lucifer threatened her a few months ago.

Mainly because this was most definitely her fault, and every demon was going to blame her for it.

How was she supposed to know the human was so pure of heart that a bloodyAngel could possess him? It wasn't fair—none of this was fair.

It was because Lucifer never told them the truth. If he was just honest that, no, they were never going to be able to open the gates to hell because God would always make up some ridiculous rule that wasn't consistent with anything else, then perhaps she wouldn't mess up as much as she did. Perhaps maybe, just maybe, they could have been less stressed and focused on something else that would help them. But no, he gave them the task of opening the gates to hell, and only then would they be free.

This was all a shame. Gwen knew it—she had called it before, and she would say it again: Lucifer was a lying bastard who deserved to be tortured for an eternity.

She didn't say this out loud, however, as she knew it would just bring her more pain even though he already had a plan lined up for her. Then perhaps she should speak her mind more. There didn't seem to be any more consequences than the ones she was already facing.

They reached the edge of the city before they stopped and looked back at whatever the heck Collin now was. He still was in Vatican City, flying up in the air.

"What is that?" James asked now that they had stopped to examine what had happened.

Gwen wasn't sure how to answer as she wasn't sure what she could say. *Oh, that's my ex, the guy you killed, now reincarnated, or whatever, into an Angel. Surprise?*

There were a couple of reasons why she didn't want to say that. First off, that was her hybrid, meaning if she died, then so did that thing. Potentially. This hadn't happened so perhaps their tie was broken and he wouldn't die if she was killed because of the Angel blood that was moving through him.

Second, they were all already mad at her for taunting him. She felt that she would be blamed for all this for a few reasons. She had made him. She didn't kill him in Moscow. She let him get away when James had him cornered moments before. Yes, she did distract James so Collin could get away. She did it in a playful way, but James knew—he always knew. Then she taunted him, and somehow Erik got this idea in his head.

Did Erik know? Gwen couldn't believe that he did, otherwise they would have done this a lot sooner. She wasn't sure, as the salt barrier was hiding his scent, but he appeared more powerful than a Gargoyles. If they knew this could happen, they would have made one a long while ago.

So he just took a shot in the dark and it worked. That was completely unfair.

"Let's head to Jerusalem," Seth said, "before that thing figures out what he is capable of. He might not know where he needs to go."

Gwen nodded although she doubted the last part. Erik had spoken to Collin before he killed himself, which probably included where he needed to go. It was pretty much a race now. But Gwen kept her mouth shut, worried that Seth might realize they could in fact kill her to try and stop Collin.

Jürgen had just mentioned doing that, so she really didn't want to bring it up. Gwen followed them as they headed toward one of the smaller local airports. It seemed that they were going to hijack a plane this time around instead of taking something commercial. Gwen wondered how many more hours in the sky she would have to be before this was all over.

As they used their quick speed to get to the closest airport, Gwen suddenly felt a rush of power coming from behind her. All of them quickly turned around to find that Collin had left the salt circle and was, luckily, heading in the opposite direction. Then she realized where he was heading—southeast toward Jerusalem.

The power she sensed—the power they all sensed— was unlike anything else she had ever felt. It was a combination of what Gargoyles smelled like with demon and something else. If Gwen had to name it, it almost felt like Lucifer, but not quite as strong or corrupt.

What exactly was possessing him? Was it an Archangel?

Gwen shuddered at the thought. There was no way he would have gained the same powers as an Archangel. Why would one of them even give him the power? It would have been against everything they stood for.

But this was war, Gwen thought. They were capable of anything.

James grabbed her hand and kept her close as they all turned to head out of there. Gwen knew it wasn't just because they had a new enemy but because the other two might try to kill her to stop Collin. She hoped that all their threats had been empty and that they wouldn't turn on her.

Just in case, though, she kept her mouth shut as they made it to the airport.

CHAPTER TWENTY-SIX

Collin didn't know what this feeling was.

When he bit into Erik, it was just like it had been any other time he fed on him, but then suddenly everything changed. It was as if his entire body was tingling with power—a power unlike any he had before. It was similar to when Gwen turned him fully into a hybrid, but times thirty. It was pure light—pure power—not corrupted by anything.

It was unreal.

His body felt as if it were going to explode, and the

light made him feel like it was on fire. All of it had rushed into him at once, and he wasn't sure if he were going to be able to handle it.

At first everything had gone white, and all Collin could do was hear a voice. Whose it was, he wasn't sure. Erik's? It was loud and told him to guard the gate with his life. He didn't argue with it, mainly because there was no point to and because he knew what was at stake.

Erik had sacrificed himself so Collin could obtain this power. As to how Erik knew this was going to happen, he wasn't sure. He doubted if he really knew or not.

Collin wasn't sure how much time had passed before he realized what was happening. He was floating above the Vatican. That was right. They were in the middle of a fight, and the demons were trying to destroy him. He peered around but didn't see any signs of them. It was smart of them to run as they probably didn't know what was going on either.

He used his senses. Gargoyles weren't able to sense where demons were, but it seemed that Collin still had that power from being a hybrid. He noticed they were heading north, probably to an airport or something to get to Jerusalem.

So that just meant Collin would have to head out of there first.

Collin could have gone after them, but he didn't want to cause more of a scene. There were a lot of humans in Rome, ones who had taken cover after they watched a battle between Heaven and hell. But the gate, however, was away from where humans lived. They could go all out there.

Erik had given Collin the coordinates before he died, but Collin found that he didn't need them. He could sense where the darkness was leaking from. Now that he wasn't focused on the light coming into him, he noticed that the world was a bit darker—as if someone used a gloomy filter over everything. Clouds appeared to be forming, bringing even more darkness.

Lucifer was getting restless. He could sense it.

There was still a lot he didn't understand about his powers, but he was finding he could sense more and more about the world. He could feel the good and evil in people.

This was way too much for a human to handle, Collin thought to himself. He wondered if the only reason he could handle it was because he was also a hybrid demon.

So the fact he had demon powers was why he could handle all this Angelic light. That was ironic. But if that were the case, then no one else in the world had ever felt the feeling he did, which excited and scared him even more.

He was over the Mediterranean Sea when it occurred to him he was flying. It had felt so natural—as if he had done it a million times.

Then it hit him—was he being possessed? Was there something else inside him that was calling the shots?

Collin wasn't sure if that made him feel better or worse. It was nice thinking that there was someone helping him, but he couldn't feel it, which frightened him. How was he supposed to figure all this out on his own? He guessed since he picked up flying so easily that perhaps he could figure out the rest just as easily.

At least that's what he hoped.

Perhaps it was Erik who was with him. That made him feel a bit better since he knew Erik. If it was another Gargoyles, he felt a bit worried. Did they think him a monster because he was once with a demon? And because he was a hybrid? These were things he knew he shouldn't worry about, but he didn't have anyone to talk this out with. He was on his own.

He was on his own.

He let those words really sink in. Collin wondered if this was what Erik felt like when Elizabeth died. Although he figured Erik felt alone, now he really truly knew what that felt like. Collin had always had the Gargoyles to rely on, and now he had no one.

Except Gwen.

But he really didn't have her on his side. If Collin were honest, she was really a point against him. And his weakness for a couple of different reasons. She could get to him, as there was a small part in his heart that still cared for her even though he knew she didn't actually care for him. Was that true, though? When they were a couple, she seemed to genuinely care about him. But now that she was back with James and her demon friends, it seemed like there was a switch and she was no longer the Gwen he knew.

Then there was the fact that if she died, he would too.

So did that mean he would have to keep her for last? Or was he no longer tied to her blood and life as he was now something completely different?

When he got to Jerusalem, perhaps he could figure it out. All he knew was that he needed to get there first, and then he could take a breath and figure out what exactly he could do. He just knew that if there were any trumpets appearing to stay clear of them. That was the instrument of the end times, and he didn't want to start that.

He was flying over Greece now, or at least that was what it looked like. He knew his European geography pretty well, and if his sense of direction was correct, which since he could sense the gate, it was, then he should be above Greece. Collin wondered how fast he was flying and why it didn't seem like he was using much power to do all this.

How powerful was he? And what did this make him?

There was no one to give him answers. Heck, he doubted the demons or the Gargoyles could have given him an answer. He was something that had never existed before. That both excited and frightened him.

But now he had to focus on how he was going to win. He had four demons to take down, and if he slipped up, then they would be able to open the gate. If Erik couldn't take the four of them down with Collin's help, how was he going to do it by himself? What special powers, besides flight, did he have? What was his purpose, and why was this happening?

He prayed he would be able to figure it out when he got to his destination; otherwise, he was going to have one heck of an explanation when he died and went to Heaven.

CHAPTER TWENTY-SEVEN

James wasn't sure if this was the worst-case scenario, but it sure felt like it.

There was a long list of things he was pissed off about, mainly the other demons. First off, Jürgen and Seth had stopped him from attacking Collin since he wasn't important. Well clearly he was. Then Gwen had distracted him when he had almost killed him once and for all.

Actually, this was all Gwen's fault. She was the one who created Collin—if she had simply let him die that night, then this wouldn't have happened. They would have probably taken down all the Gargoyles by now. But that wasn't what happened. No, she had to have some sort of feeling for that stupid human, and now they were in this horrible situation.

So no matter who he wanted to blame, it didn't solve anything. They needed to work together to take down whatever that was.

They had grabbed a pilot, turned him into a minion, and now were flying out to Jerusalem on a Cessna. They would have to make a stop or two, depending on how much fuel this plane held. James glanced down to find they were already almost at the heel of the boot and he could see the Caribbean Sea in the distance.

How far had Collin gotten? Was he flying the entire way to the gates? Or did he stop somewhere? Or was he waiting to attack them and knock them out of the sky, where they were sitting ducks as they couldn't fly? They might not have died from the crash as long as they didn't start a fire, but it would weaken them tremendously, and then he could kill them.

But he didn't see any sign of Collin. They were

lucky. He must have been given orders to go straight there, and since he didn't understand the power he possessed, it was more than likely he didn't think about different ways to take them out. Simple human only thought simple thoughts.

James leaned back and put his arm around Gwen. She hadn't moved a muscle but was staring out the window. She felt stiff, as if ready for any kind of attack. Whether she was worried about Collin attacking or Seth and Jürgen teaming up on her, he wasn't sure.

"Penny for your thoughts?" he whispered into her ear.

She jumped a little, as if she had totally detached from the world around her. "Oh, I don't know. My mind is just wandering."

"Thinking about what the heck happened?"

"Aren't you? I didn't even know it was possible… He turned into something else. What now? What does this mean?"

James didn't know the answer to that—he doubted anyone did. "It means we just have one more obstacle to defeat, and then we will be set. Look at the sky, Gwen. It is already turning dark. We can still open the gates without killing him, as long as we distract him long enough."

Gwen took a deep breath and let it out slowly. "Yeah, that might be our best bet, huh? Once the door is open, then Lucifer himself can take care of that thing."

That was a good point. If they were fast enough, something else could take care of Collin. James glanced back at Seth.

"You're quiet. What is our plan, O captain, my captain?"

Seth gave James a look but answered the question. "What you just said. Two of us are going to distract Collin, and the other two are going to try to open the door."

"What, are we going to draw straws or something?"

Seth folded his arms. "I'm still deciding how to team everyone up. I don't trust either of you two to do the job, so I'm in a bit of a bind."

"We will take Collin," Gwen said. "It's the best battle strategy."

"You aren't calling the shots."

"He will want me dead last, just in case my death does kill him, although at this point I don't think it will. And James wants him dead more than anyone. The two of us are the best pick to take him down."

"But will you take him down? That's the real question," Jürgen growled. "I think we should kill you now and see if he does die."

James glared at him. "Do it, and you will die before your hand touches Gwen."

"Enough!" Seth ordered as he leaned back in his seat. "Fine. The two of you will distract Collin, and Jürgen and I will prepare the ceremony to open the gates. But if there is any funny business, I will let Jürgen end Gwen. You understand? No betraying us."

Gwen eyed Seth but said nothing. James wasn't sure what she was thinking, but he had a feeling she was starting to doubt all this. As she said, there always seemed to be something that was stopping them. But they were close. This was just one more person to kill. And that was what they did best—kill.

"You won't need to. We will take care of that hybrid once and for all. He can't be that strong—at least, no stronger than a Gargoyles."

None of them responded to that remark, and James wasn't sure he believed it himself. Collin had shone so brightly—was he simply like a Gargoyles or was he something more? Did he still have the powers of a demon? And if that was the case, he had all the good qualities of both creatures and didn't have any weaknesses.

Other than that human heart of his.

Although Collin was similar to Gargoyles in that he cared about humans, his heart was a bit different in that he loved Gwen. They could use that, just as Gwen had been using that again and again to twist him round her finger.

If he still cared for her. The way he looked at her when she cut her finger to let her scent linger in the air said that he did. But that was before this holy light. Perhaps his heart no longer belonged to her. But even if they didn't have that against him, James didn't think it would be too much trouble for the two of them to take him down.

They still had their weapons that they had grabbed from the gladiator school Gwen had found. He was still rather pissed that Seth didn't give them weapons in the beginning so that he could surprise attack Erik. It didn't work, and they had to get their own swords. It surprised James how good Erik was at the sword still. It had been years since he clashed weapons with Erik. Having a good opponent used to be one of his favorite things, but now he just wanted all his enemies dead.

Then he and Gwen could have a nice beach house somewhere warm and spend the rest of eternity together.

He kissed the top of her head, and she turned to him and smiled gently. She leaned her head on his shoulder and kept staring out the window. He wondered if it was because she liked to see where she was going, or if she was worried that Collin was actually going to attack.

Or perhaps she was spacing as she figured out a strategy to betray them all.

No, she wouldn't do that to him. Not again. She was probably serious when she said that she didn't mean to distract him when he had almost killed Collin earlier. She was bringing weapons and had simply arrived and announced what she was carrying.

The more he thought about it, the more it ate him up inside. Was she really still trying to help him after all this time? Did she really look him in the eyes and swear she would destroy Collin but only lied to James again and again?

He needed to calm down before he made a scene on this plane. There were only demons on this plane, but they were demons who wanted Gwen destroyed. If he made it obvious that not even he trusted her, then they would try to kill her. He doubted they could, as Gwen was quick, smart, and both of them were stronger with their blood bond.

James moved a bit of Gwen's hair from her neck. She turned to him with a grin.

"You know they hate it when they see us feed off each other, right?"

"Yes, but I am tired and need a drink."

She moved the rest of her hair out of the way. "Fine, take a drink."

James bit into her neck as he heard Jürgen make gagging noises. He ignored him, as he took in a bit of Gwen's blood.

And yet, somewhere in his chest, he felt as if this was going to be the last time he ever would be able to.

CHAPTER
TWENTY-EIGHT

They made two stops to fill up for fuel on their way to Jerusalem.

It was tiresome, but they couldn't really go on a big flight as they wanted to discuss what to do next without looks or dealing with humans in general. During fueling, however, they killed some time and fed on some humans. Now all four of them were full, strong, and ready to fight.

The problem was, which made Gwen laugh, none of them remembered where the gate was outside

Jerusalem.

Gwen was still giggling to herself, and Seth went to fetch them a car. He was able to get his hands on an open-aired Jeep. They knew the darkness was spilling out of the gate as all the demons in hell were gathering and waiting to be released, but they couldn't quite pinpoint where that was.

So Gwen laughed. And laughed. And laughed.

"Will you just shut it, or I will do it myself?" Jürgen growled.

She tried to hold it back, but it was just so funny. They couldn't remember where the most important thing in the world was to them. It was hilarious.

"I'm sorry, but like, can you blame me? After all this, none of us can remember the tomb where the Son of God was held—the tomb that released demons for three days and three nights. Lucifer is probably livid watching us right now."

Jürgen threw a punch at her, but Gwen jumped back, causing Jürgen to stumble a little.

"Stand still!"

"Nope!"

She ran around James, who did his best not to get punched himself by Jürgen. He was having fun as well as Gwen saw him smile.

"Will you two knock it off! Get in the car!"

All three of them did as they were told, and Gwen jumped in the back next to James. She gave him a kiss, then turned to look out at the scenery.

Jerusalem had changed a bit since the last time she was there. She tried to remember when it was. Perhaps the Crusades? If that was the case, then it really had been a long time. It appeared like any other city in the world, full of cars and neglect for the natural scenery around it, because humans thought advancing their kind was through mastering nature. They had no idea that they had no power over nature, and if the demons didn't destroy them first, then it would be nature.

Silly humans thinking they had any power.

The farther Seth drove, the more deserted the area looked. Although the desert wasn't a bad place—actually Gwen found it to be fun because only the strongest survived out here—Gwen preferred a nice tropical beach where she and James could play in the sand together. Soon they would get to retire, of sorts, and be together forever. She couldn't wait for that.

Except that would mean she would have to take down Collin.

She didn't like this part of the plan. Although she knew they had to, as he had sided with the Gargoyles, she really didn't want to. It was her fault that he had gotten involved with all this. She just wanted to restore his life and make him human again.

But that was impossible. There was no way he could go back to his human life—especially since now he was some weird Angel-demon-human thing. She needed to stop protecting him and put him out of his misery.

Her heart cringed at the thought. They had spent so much time together in London—time she cherished as it made her feel human and for once forget what was waiting for her in hell. For those memories, she didn't want to let Collin suffer, but they were well past that point. He was suffering. Or at least he used to be. Now it seemed like he was all-powerful.

Which did not bode well for Gwen.

The odds were the link was severed because of whatever happened when he killed Erik or was drinking his blood when Erik killed himself. But there was still the possibility that if the other demons killed Gwen, Collin would die. And she didn't like that fact.

Luckily she had James with her, which meant the other two would back off as the odds were even. Gwen had no problem killing Jürgen and Seth in self-defense, and she had a feeling neither did James.

"So where are we going if you don't know where the gate is?"

"No back seat drivers!" Seth exclaimed.

Gwen leaned forward so that she was closer to Seth. "No, seriously. Where are you heading if you don't even know where to go? I mean, it would be one thing if we could sense it, but it feels like darkness is coming from every which way possible."

"Gwen, I swear to Lucifer, I will pull this Jeep over and end you. Got that?"

She shrugged and leaned back in her chair. James placed his hand on her leg. "Don't worry, my love. We will find it. Seth and Jürgen are on it."

Seth slammed on his breaks, and Gwen and James crashed into the seats in front of them.

"Fuck! What did you do that for?" James exclaimed.

Seth hit the gas again. "Both of you just shut up!"

James mouthed something to Gwen, which she figured was along the lines of, "somebody is bitchy."

Gwen grinned and mouthed back, "I know, right?"

They traveled to the edge of the city. They at least knew it wouldn't be anywhere within the city as they recalled it being way out in the middle of nowhere. Even with the sprawling of cities and human settlements in general, the eerie energy that came off the place made humans subconsciously stay away from it.

In general, or at least last time she was in Jerusalem, she could sense it. Now, however, as the aura seemed to be coming from every direction, it made it impossible to find the source.

What she should have been able to sense was Collin. He had lost a lot of blood, not to mention he had a strange aura after Erik gave him his life. But with all the darkness leaking through, everything was masked. It was like a thick fog had surrounded them all and they couldn't tell which way was up or down.

It was exciting to say the least.

Is this how the world would always feel now? Or was this just a taste of the darkness that would pour out of the gates once they opened? It felt strange to Gwen as she knew her aura matched this feeling, and yet it felt foreign.

Like it shouldn't belong.

Gwen noted that Seth had taken them east of the city. Gwen bit her lip, wanting to comment that she remembered it being south. But he had said no back seat drivers, so she kept her mouth shut. It gave Collin more time to figure out how to take down all four.

She had a feeling he would leave her for last, just in case he was still tied to her. Which meant it was up to her to take him down. She didn't like that thought, but it was the only way they could open the gates—they had to do something. Or else Lucifer would punish them in hell.

That is if what he said was true. Perhaps hell wasn't that, and there was no torture like he said. Who was Gwen kidding? That was probably the only thing that was true in all of this. But whether they would still be tortured when they opened the gates was a possibility just because he could.

Gwen knew she needed to stop thinking like that, but she couldn't help it. Curveballs kept being thrown into the mix, and she couldn't help but worry what would really happen when they opened the gates. But did they have a choice? It wasn't like she couldn't or else she would be punished, but it seemed like it was an impossible task. Heaven kept making rules up, and they couldn't do anything but obey.

Only time would tell now as the gate had been

unlocked and all they had to do was perform the ceremony to open it. After they found it, that was.

CHAPTER TWENTY-NINE

So this was it.

Collin stood in the middle of nowhere in front of a cave. There was a large rock to the side, but most of the area was covered in overgrown foliage now. If he couldn't sense the demonic presence of the gate there, he wouldn't have even noticed it.

It was surreal to him that this was where Jesus was buried. He had seen documentaries where archeologists talked about the possible places, but this was definitely not on the list. Was he the first human to find this place in centuries?

Who was he kidding? He wasn't human any longer. He was some mashup of a demon andAngel. He peered down to his hands that still glowed. Was this like when a player in *Super Smash Bros.* got the star? Would it suddenly end at the most inopportune time?

No, this wasn't a video game. He could tell the energy was there, and it was going to stay—at least until the fight was over. Collin peered around. This would be the perfect spot as there were no humans who would get in the middle of the mess. He didn't have to hold back.

He knew he could fly, and he had superspeed and could locate where the demons were, but besides that he wasn't sure what he could do. He felt stronger but wasn't sure how to test this. He glanced around and found a large boulder. Bracing himself for how much it possibly could hurt, he punched the boulder.

Collin didn't feel a thing as the boulder exploded into a million pieces. He had never imagined he could be so strong. It was as if he were a superhero or something. Taking a deep breath, he tried not to geek out and jump up.

Was there anything else? he asked himself. He

figured there wouldn't be as it wasn't like the Gargoyles had many powers besides what he already tried. He didn't have lasers or control over elements— at least, he didn't feel like he did. Having the ability to fly, locate the demons, and superstrength would be enough for him to take them down.

He was beginning to feel better about it all already.

Now he just had to wait for them. He closed his eyes and focused on where the demons were. He furrowed his brows as he noticed they seemed to be heading in the wrong direction. Why was that? Was there something he was missing?

Opening his eyes, he peered at the gate. This was definitely it. He couldn't see it with his mind, per se, but he could sense that it was here. So where were the demons heading? Did they have some kind of stash they were going to first? Were they gathering weapons or minions? Collin didn't like this development and wanted the fight to be over with. He was ready—hyped up on whatever energy was possessing him.

He thought about going and surprise attacking them. Would it be smart to do so before they gathered whatever they were looking for? Or was it trap for him to go and check out? He decided it would be best to wait here as this was the location they would be eventually heading. He would just have to find out later what they were gathering.

Collin took a seat and closed his eyes in meditation. Would he be able to hear that voice again if he closed his eyes and listened? He took a few deep, calming breaths. He could sense all the energy around him— darkness mainly as it seeped out of the cracks of the gate. Collin tried not to focus on it as he felt like it was trying to draw him in. He was stronger than it, he told himself. He couldn't let it deter what he was trying to accomplish.

The problem was that it was everywhere. The more he sat there, the stronger the feeling of darkness became. It was suffocating, and before he knew it, he could hear whispers.

"Open the gate—obtain immortality and eternal paradise."

"We will grant any wish, just do as we ask."

"You could have Gwen all to yourself if you just listened."

He flinched at the last one. Whatever was trying to speak to him noticed. "Oh, so that is what you want. Gwen all to yourself."

Collin didn't answer as he knew deep down it was what he wanted. But that was before he found out she was a demon—that was before he found out the truth of what was going on. When she was a human, however, he wanted a long life with her. He wanted to open the pub with her, have children, grow old, and even see the world. Now he just wanted her destroyed so he could be done with this curse.

"But is that what you really want? If you help us, we can give you a normal life."

Collin didn't like where this was going. Because deep down he really did want all that. He wanted a normal life, but would he want it at the price of the entire world?

"No, you won't. You are promising lies—lies that wouldn't even come true. I have seen the destruction the demons have done. Even if I was willing to destroy this world for what I wanted, I know that you would never fulfill your end of the bargain."

There was laughter. It was eerie and deep and didn't sound like anything in this world.

"You are sure full of yourself for being a human. What makes you think I don't have the power to fulfill your wishes, hmm?"

Collin knew he should ignore the voice, especially since he had a feeling he knew who it was. He had heard the voice once before, and it was still fresh in his mind. "Because otherwise Gwen would never have tried to look for redemption. Her love for James was strong enough for her to fall from Heaven, but the reason she wanted it all to end was the fact she knew she wasn't ever going to get what she wanted. Everything she promised were lies, and she was sick of doing your bidding."

The darkness around him felt as if it had started a fire. Collin didn't feel as if he were burning, however, but more as if this demon was trying to show his power.

As if Lucifer was trying to threaten him.

"You don't know what I am capable of! You don't know the power I possess! My Twelve Generals have not fulfilled their duties and therefore have not received their promises!"

"If you fulfill their promises, then the promise you are offering me is not possible. You cannot fulfill both James and Gwen's promise and the one I want. So yes, you are full of empty promises and lies."

Collin didn't dare open his eyes even though it almost felt as if Lucifer was standing behind him. He gulped as he pissed off one of the most powerful beings in all Heaven and hell. He could feel the creature's breath on his skin.

"I could have given you paradise, but instead you chose hell. When the gates open, don't think you will be getting away with this—don't think you will be going to Heaven. No hybrids have ever escaped my grasp. No, the moment Gwen bit you, your soul was damned to hell for an eternity. I will destroy your soul —shatter it into a million pieces and bring it back into creation again and again. If you thought Gwen was sadistic in how she handled you, you haven't seen anything yet."

Was that true? Was he really damned to hell because of what Gwen did? He felt the horror and hate start to fill his chest.

And then he noticed the darkness around him was bombarding his aura.

It was a lie to get him to falter. Collin shook his head. "No, you are a liar. I don't believe that is true. Even if it were, I wouldn't turn my back on the Gargoyles and what is good in the world. The world needs me, and I am willing to pay whatever the price."

The darkness subsided, and Collin took a large

breath. That felt close—closer than he wanted to admit. Collin's eyes flickered open to find that he was still in front of the cave. He had tried to meditate to speak to Erik or someone and talked to Lucifer instead. Either way, he had the answers he needed—he had to defeat the demons once and for all to finally rid this world of all the darkness that was Lucifer.

CHAPTER THIRTY

James had to agree with Gwen. It was rather hilarious they didn't know where they were going.

When was the last time he had seen the gate? He tried to remember. Was it during the Crusades? Or had it been more recently? If it were more recently, he felt that he would have remembered where it was.

It didn't help that darkness and evil were clouding everything around them, and James felt like he was in a fog and didn't know which way was up. He could barely sense the three demons in the Jeep with him due to all the power. It was nerve-racking, and he hoped that Collin was having the same problems as them locating where they were.

For some reason he doubted that was the case.

The beings in Heaven liked to throw them curveballs, which was not fair to say the least. Collin shouldn't be this powerful, and Erik shouldn't have been able to give his life force like that to the kid. If that was what happened. He still wasn't sure what he saw or what was going on. He just hoped that the human ran out of juice and was passed out somewhere or drowning in the middle of the ocean.

But he was never that lucky. None of them were ever that lucky.

So they just had one more strange creature to take down. It was no biggie. All four of them were powerful as they had taken a pit stop and filled up on some humans. They were at their fullest power and would destroy the hybrid before he even knew what was coming.

Seth this time had acquired some swords for them all along with some guns. Although it did feel a bit cheap using guns to take kill someone, it was their only option to slow the hybrid down. They had to use whatever means they had to open the gates, or else they were going to find only torture awaiting them.

James shook off the fear he had for Lucifer. All of them were afraid of the king of hell. They had seen what he was capable in the war with Heaven. They didn't want to be on his bad side.

Except Gwen, of course. She seemed to want to be on everyone's bad side.

But James wouldn't let her fuck this up. They couldn't, because if she tried anything to help Collin, he had a feeling Seth and Jürgen would snap and kill her to see if it took out Collin as well. James doubted it would, but he wasn't going to let the two hurt his girl—not after all this time.

They could count on Collin being afraid of killing Gwen for that same reason, however, and use it to their advantage. They could put Gwen on the front lines, making Collin hesitate. It would be the best tactic in taking him out, and James wasn't afraid of Gwen getting a little bruised up. She would recover in no time flat. They just had to use whatever means necessary to open the gates.

James and Gwen were going to try to take Collin on by themselves while Seth and Jürgen tried to take on opening the gate. James hoped he could take Collin down himself as it would be sweet revenge on the human touching his girl. He wanted more than anything to rip out that hybrid's throat.

But first they needed to find the damn place. James tapped on the door, trying to think. When they came to Jerusalem last time, they had come from the north. They had battled a few Gargoyles on the opposite side of the city…

So the gate was more than likely to the south.

James leaned forward to Seth. "I think it's to the south."

"What makes you so certain?" Seth growled.

"Because when we came to Jerusalem last time, it was from the north and we went straight through the city."

Seth was silent for a moment, as if he were trying to recall that battle. Suddenly the car turned right and James almost flew out the side.

"Watch it!" James yelled.

"You wouldn't have died."

"No, but it would have hurt!"

Gwen smiled at him. He didn't know why, but he had a feeling that she had realized it was to the south a while ago but kept her mouth shut to spite Seth. He had told her to stop talking, so he couldn't blame her.

They headed south, and the farther they went south, the darker it seemed to be. That was a good sign. The darkness had to be pouring out of the gate as the locks, so to speak, were gone. Each of the Gargoyles were like a separate lock that only came undone when they died. With the last one gone, it was now unlocked and they could open it through the proper rituals.

James wasn't even going to ask Seth or Jürgen if they remembered the ritual, mainly because it would show that James couldn't remember what Satan had told them to do. It was some kind of chant and their blood, if he was correct. The door only needed one demon's blood. That way, as long as one demon was alive, that meant they could open the gate.

It was starting to look somewhat familiar to him as the skyline hadn't changed. The plants had, and there were many buildings behind them that were new. Many, many buildings. But in the wilderness it was quite the same.

He couldn't wait until the humans were gone and they could enjoy all the wilderness. This world was beautiful, and yet these humans kept destroying it for their own selfish greed. Even demons weren't that cruel. There were a lot of things humans did to each other that demons wouldn't even dream of.

Once they got closer, James could sense Collin. He had already found it, either because he for some reason could sense it all better than the demons, which was nerve-racking, or because Erik told him exactly where it was. It would seem that the Gargoyles knew where it was. Perhaps they had better memory, or perhaps, since this was a holy land, so to speak, they remembered where it was. And it had been where their so-called Lord came back to life.

James remembered that day like it was yesterday, even though he couldn't quite remember where the tomb was. They had thought they defeated the Son of God to find out they only got three days' reign over the world. Then all the demons and darkness went back into the gates of hell, and they had to start all over.

Lucifer had said they won—Lucifer told them they had free rein and didn't need to work any longer. Then all that disappeared from their grasp.

He wondered if they would in fact have it happen again. Would their reign only last for a couple of days? Weeks? Years? Perhaps Gwen was right in thinking that there would be more to it.

No. He couldn't have these thoughts. He had to keep going. They had to finish this.

The closer they got to the tomb, the stronger the presence of Collin became. None of them said a word, but James could tell by their silence that they didn't like what they were sensing.

He was both a demon and an Angel—but not just a Gargoyles. No, he had the same sense of an Archangel.

James had only met an Archangel once. It was a long, long time ago, before this tomb existed. Archangels would come down to the world and smite any city they realized had been overrun by minions. It wasn't fair, but nothing about this war had been fair. They were strong —much stronger than any Gargoyles, which was why this was so disturbing.

Who was possessing Collin? How was that even possible?

It was more than likely Michael, as Michael liked to get involved with the affairs of man more than any other Archangel. One thing was for certain, however, and that was the fact that there was never an instance that any demon had won against an Archangel.

But Collin wasn't really an Archangel—he just had

some of their powers. It was more than likely that he was only given some of the powers and they didn't have to worry about any trumpets or Collin waving a hand over a city and it completely turning into salt. No, it was probably a hoax—something to scare them off from the gate.

Or this was going to go completely south and they were screwed.

James tried to stay positive, but it was harder with each and every passing moment. He did not like the energy coming off Collin and hoped that Collin had no idea what kind of powers he possessed. Knowing that human, James figured he was probably right.

He turned to Gwen, who appeared as perplexed. What they had felt in Rome was correct, and they had quite an enemy to defeat. She glanced at him and smiled a little.

"This battle is going to hurt, isn't it?" she whispered. He wasn't sure if she meant physically or emotionally. Either way.

He nodded. "Yup. But we will win. We have to."

He didn't say anything as they could now see the gate in the distance and, in front of it, Collin waiting.

And then he started running straight toward them, his

fist back as if he were going to punch the Jeep.

Great. He had realized how strong he was. This was not going to end well.

CHAPTER THIRTY-ONE

Gwen leaped from the Jeep as Collin came crashing into it.

As long as he didn't have the other powers of an Archangel, they had a chance. She doubted they were going to randomly give him the ability to wipe an entire city off the face of the Earth, but at this point, she didn't know what the creatures in Heaven were thinking. All she knew was that they cheated just like they always did, and this was not fair. There were too many surprises, and she hated surprises. She should be the only one making chaos—not the good guys. Wasn't there a rule about that?

The Jeep exploded into a million pieces. She sighed, as she really liked that style Jeep. They just didn't make them like they used to. Gwen glanced over at James to make sure he was fine. He landed on his own two feet. She didn't check on Seth or Jürgen as she didn't care if they did or not. They had a mission, and they would figure it out. James and Gwen had their own mission.

"Collin," she called out. "I see you got a bit stronger. And lighter? Like, you are glowing. Literally."

He shrugged. "You know, I work out and all that."

"Right. Nothing to do with that whole Erik killing himself thing."

"Perhaps I just leveled up really fast." Collin appeared in front of her faster than she could register. He punched her straight in the stomach, and she went flying back.

Hot damn, she thought. That hurt. A lot. She smacked into the side of a rock and bounced off. The rock was cracked. She slowly got up and spat out blood.

"Oh, now I really want to taste your blood." She felt her eyes turn yellow, and she went straight for Collin. He was ready to block her punch when she switched gears, so to speak, and pulled out her pistol. She shot a round at him, all of the bullets embedding into his skin. He didn't even flinch. She jumped back and landed next to James.

She leaned her head and whispered into his ear. "I think we are fucked."

He sarcastically smiled. "Yeah, I think you might be right."

Collin came straight at them, ready to punch both of them. The two demons jumped back, pulling out their swords. Collin wasn't armed, more than likely because he didn't think he needed to be. The bullets didn't seem to do anything to him, but perhaps swords would.

"For the record"—Gwen turned to James—"I told you this was going to go south for some stupid reason."

"Yeah, yeah. I know."

Gwen swung at Collin, and Collin stepped out of the way faster than she could even recognize. This was unfair—she was supposed to be faster than a Gargoyles. How was Collin faster than she was? And was this what humans felt like before she murdered them in cold blood? It sucked.

She swung again and again, and Collin was able to move out of the way of each and every strike. Maybe he was right—maybe he didn't need weapons, and he just needed himself.

"I have to ask, Collin," she said, almost out of breath. "Which Archangel is possessing you right now?"

"You know," he commented as he grabbed the wrist that she was holding the sword with. "I really don't know. But you can let go of that sword now."

"I really don't want to. I like my sword. Makes me feel like a pirate."

He laughed. "A pirate, huh? Let me guess, Blackbeard? Anne Bonny?"

Gwen could see James sneaking up behind Collin. She nodded. "Perhaps. Some of the pirates were actually Gargoyles as well. They weren't going after gold but trying to take us down."

"Sounds like something they would do. Oh, also, you better hold on."

Gwen's eyes went wide as Collin flew up in the air. She had forgotten he could do that. She let out a scream and dropped her sword.

"Demons really don't like heights, do they? The Gargoyles always seemed to enjoy taking them up in the clouds. I didn't quite understand it, but now that I can, I totally get it. It's fun to make your kind scream for your life."

Was he always this sadistic? Or was the Archangel also taking over his mind? Gwen added, "Don't forget, our kind is chained to the Earth. The higher we go up, the more the chains yank on our bodies."

His eyes widened. "Right, that tattoo of yours is a real chain. It must hurt like hell to go on a plane."

"That it does. First order of business after opening the gates of hell is to destroy all planes. I hate them."

He laughed. "That's such an honest comment. For that, how about I let you down?"

Before she could protest, he dropped her.

Gwen went down like a bag of bricks—even more so with the force of the chains pulling her down as well. She screamed—tears being wiped away by the air that was rushing past her ears. She watched as the ground came closer and closer.

The impact wouldn't kill her, but it would hurt. And she wouldn't be getting up anytime soon. It would take a bit to heal back up, and then Collin could kill her. She had really doubted he would go after her first like this, but it was clear that she was wrong.

She was mere feet from the ground when she felt something hit her straight in the side. Instead of hitting the ground, she was now flying sideways, back into the rock at speeds she didn't know was possible. As Gwen fumbled in the air, she saw that Collin had flown down and was the one who dealt the kick. Lucky her.

Gwen hit the side of the slight hill, crushing and indenting the once-solid rock at least a few feet. She found that she couldn't get up. Collin stepped up to her and squared down.

"Stay there for a bit. I need to take care of the rest of you demons before finishing you off."

She weakly made a thumbs-up, as she knew she wasn't getting up anytime soon. James was running their way, and she wanted to scream for him to run— get as far away as he could. Collin wasn't messing around.

But James didn't listen to her internal shouts and now possessed two swords, more than likely picking up the one she had dropped, and swung both at Collin. Collin ducked out of the way and kicked James's legs out from under him. James luckily was able to get up before Collin could land his foot on his stomach. James swung sword after sword at Collin, but Collin was able to move out of the way for each and every one of them.

Gwen blinked slowly, as everything was still a daze

and her ears were ringing. She could see in the distance that Jürgen and Seth were starting the ceremony. Perhaps Gwen and James could distract Collin long enough for them to finish. How long did it take again? She couldn't remember and was glad that she wasn't in charge of that as she would have failed miserably.

She took a deep breath and tried to focus on James. How long was he going to last? Collin wouldn't hesitate in killing him as his blood wasn't tied to her. Gwen couldn't let that happen, however, as James meant the world to her.

Gwen tried to move, but her entire body hurt. Taking a deep breath, she focused on her fingers and toes first. She couldn't even move those.

"Shit," she whispered. Her vision was going in and out, and Collin and James's fight was getting blurry. James seemed to be holding his own, so at least there was that. She closed her eyes for a moment.

Why was this happening? Was this all her karma coming back to haunt her? She didn't care what happened to her, but she wanted to be able to get up and save James. He didn't deserve what was waiting for him in hell. No, he deserved the paradise he was thriving to achieve.

A paradise with her.

Gwen felt the ability to move her fingers and toes.

She had to be able to move, but there were no humans within miles of there. She didn't have a car or a savior or some Archangel to come down and save her.

Then it occurred to her—dark energy was leaking out of the gates of hell. Could she tap into that? Could she heal herself from that?

She took a deep breath in and focused on tapping into that energy. She felt as if a lightning bolt had hit her. She gasped as she felt her wounds begin to heal.

The fight was just getting started.

CHAPTER THIRTY-TWO

Collin sensed her before she was upon him.

He spun around and blocked Gwen's kick. He wasn't able to keep his stance, however, as he was thrown back a bit. She had powered up somehow. If he was correct in what he sensed, she had tapped into the energy that was coming out of the gate.

She was smart, but he already knew that. That was why he tried to take her out first.

"The gate!" Gwen yelled at James. "Tap into the energy of the gate."

Collin saw confusion on James's face for a moment.

"I'll hold Collin off while you figure it out." She laughed as she took one of the swords from James.

This couldn't be good.

She was faster and stronger, but not quite as fast and strong as he was, for which he was thankful. He really did wish he knew what Archangel was possessing him, but he never got any answers when he asked. He ducked out of the way as Gwen swung at his head. Was she trying to decapitate him? He supposed that would be one way to kill him.

Collin flew up in the sky and peered down, wondering what he should do first. He glanced at the other two demons and realized he had completely forgotten about them as he was taking his anger out on James and Gwen.

He flew down straight at them. Their attention had been on the gate, but they had noticed his descent and spun around and started shooting bullets straight at him.

"Damn it," Collin said as he tried to dodge them. The bullets didn't seem to slow him down energywise, but they hurt. A lot. Before Seth and Jürgen could unload their guns on him, Gwen had caught up.

"Wait, don't leave me out of the fun!" she yelled as

she raised her sword and came down on him.

He jumped out of the way but not quite fast enough. The sword caught his skin and ripped the flesh off his shoulder. He let out a cry in pain. Gwen's eyes went wide, as if she had smelled the most delicious meal ever.

Gwen licked her blade, a few drops of his blood dripping down the steel. Her eyes glowed yellow.

Suddenly Gwen grabbed her chest as if she were having a heart attack. She screamed.

"You idiot!" Jürgen yelled at her. "We can't drink the blood of an Archangel!"

That was strange. Why couldn't they? They had drunk the blood of Gargoyles all the time. Was it different? Were Archangels too powerful for them? It didn't matter as now that left the other two open as Gwen dealt with whatever was going on with her.

Collin had spoken too soon as James had come running over with his own sword. At least it was only three to one instead of four.

The bullets began raining down on him again, and Collin flew up in the air. He had an advantage in the air as he could take a break and think about his next move, but he couldn't do much for attacking as he didn't have any weapons. Collin glanced around. It appeared that Jürgen and Seth were performing some sort of ceremony to open the gate. He would have to focus on those two first. He had been stupid not to notice what they were doing earlier, but he really just wanted to take Gwen out.

If James had listened to Gwen, that meant he was stronger now. James had been giving Collin trouble already, so he wasn't too happy that he had also powered up. He had no idea about the other two demons, but both of them had given Erik a lot of trouble, so they were more than likely equally strong. And each had weapons.

"Well, here goes nothing."

Collin dived down to where the demons were trying to open the gate. They aimed their guns and tried to shoot him. He didn't falter, swerving right and left, trying to maneuver around the bullets, or at least as much as he could. He was still getting hit left and right, but it did not hurt nearly as bad as it had when he was a hybrid. He couldn't imagine how much it would have hurt when he was just a human.

Both Seth and Jürgen ran out of bullets, and Collin heard them curse as he came slamming into them. They tried to jump out of the way, but it was too late—Collin was able to punch them both, and they went flying back into the side of the tomb. Gwen and James were running toward him, yelling.

"Use the energy of the gate! You can heal that way!"

This was turning into a movie where one person was overly powerful but then all the others become as overly powerful. Collin decided it would be best to try to take them out before they could figure out what Gwen and Collin were saying.

Another round of bullets hit into Collin's side. Collin turned to find that James also had a gun. He was surprised he hadn't used it earlier, but Collin figured it was because he had both hands occupied with swords.

Speaking of which, Collin ducked as Gwen swung straight at his head. "Are you trying to cut off my head, Gwen?"

"Perhaps. I figured it was the best bet to kill you."

"Oh, you want to kill me now? You didn't want James killing me before."

"That was before your blood almost made me burn inside out. I feel better now, though."

He stepped out of the way as she tried to slice him again and again. "Oh darn. Wouldn't it have been ironic if my blood did you in?"

"Very! I would have died laughing."

James shot another round at Collin, but Collin was able to move out of the way fast enough. Collin turned his attention to him. "Doesn't it piss you off that she brought me back to life?"

"Oh, more than you know. I just hope I get to do you in one last time."

Collin smiled as he jumped up in the air. He peered down and found that Seth and Jürgen were starting to come back around. He acted too slow—he could have probably taken them out if it weren't for Gwen and James showing up. He was starting to see why the Gargoyles liked to try to take them out one at a time. They were a pest when there were more than one, not to mention Gwen was random and cocky in general.

"Give up, Collin!" Gwen shouted. "You can't take us all down, not when the Gargoyles are gone and we don't need to kill you to open the gate!"

No, they just needed to distract him. Collin took a deep breath. He wasn't sure what he needed to do first —take out Gwen and James, at least to the point where they weren't moving, or go after the other two who were trying to open the gate. It seemed that James and

Gwen weren't going to let that happen, however.

So he would just need to take them out.

He dove back down. First, he needed to get a weapon for himself. All four of them had swords, but it would be easiest to take one from the two who already had them in their hands. Collin wondered how much it would hurt to just grab them by the blade and then pull. He had been hit by a plethora of bullets, but he found that, due to whatever was possessing him, he was able to heal rather fast.

So it didn't hurt to try.

Gwen didn't have a gun in her other hand, so he figured she would be the easiest to take the gun from.

She grinned widely when he came at her, as if she loved the fun. She appeared like a cat when it saw a mouse running toward it. He was no mouse, however, and she would learn that very soon.

Gwen swung the sword at him, but instead of dodging it, he stuck his hand out and grabbed it. Something he didn't think about because either he didn't realize how sharp the sword was or because it was a heat-of-the-moment sort of thing, but it almost sliced his right hand off. Luckily, it didn't, but it came close. Gwen just stared at him, in shock.

It was the pause he needed.

With his other hand, he grabbed the hilt out of her hand and jumped back, waiting for his hand to heal.

She started laughing. "Well, this makes things far more interesting."

Using her quick speed, she went and took a sword from Seth. He tried to protest but was still weak. She and James raised their weapons and were ready for whatever Collin had in store for them.

They each came at him on either side, and Collin jumped up in the sky, and James and Gwen almost sliced each other. This brought a small grin to his face as he turned and dived down at James. He swung at James, but James deflected each and every attack. Gwen pounced at him from the side, but Collin spun around and sliced at her. He nicked her cheek. A trail of blood fell down her face.

And it was the first time in quite some time that Collin didn't crave Gwen's blood.

Come to think about it, he didn't crave any blood at all. Was that because he was being possessed by an Archangel, or because he didn't need it any longer after taking in all of Erik's blood? Those were questions he knew he wasn't going to get answered anytime soon.

Gwen touched her blood and licked her fingers. She didn't say anything, but her face was curious, as if she noticed he didn't react to it. She smiled a little, as if she had a plan.

CHAPTER THIRTY-THREE

James noticed it—Collin didn't flinch when he saw Gwen's blood.

Did that mean they were no longer connected? Did that mean Gwen could just kill him because he was no longer her hybrid? It didn't matter to him, however, as he wanted him dead no matter what.

James swung his sword at him, but Collin jumped back a few hops, a little higher than what a normal person could do due to his wings. The wings were invisible, like the Gargoyles' had been, for the most part, but these were as if they didn't exist. James didn't feel them or see them. So was he flying without wings? Even Archangels had wings.

All this was a mystery.

What Collin was experiencing was impossible, and yet here he was—doing the impossible. It was sickening to say the least. He had power that wasn't allowed to James. He had love that wasn't allowed to James. He had redemption that wasn't allowed to James. Collin had everything that James wanted—had everything without having to sell himself.

It wasn't fair—especially since those in Heaven gave him most of it.

Collin jumped toward James, and James blocked the attack. James would have been getting a bit tired if it weren't for the fact that they could take in the energy seeping out of the gate. James hoped that Jürgen and Seth would be getting up soon and helping them fight. They would need all four to take Collin down.

But they could still open the gate with Collin here, so there was that. If the doors to hell opened, then Lucifer could deal with Collin.

James would pay to see that.

So perhaps they should keep him alive so he didn't

simply die and go to Heaven. No, if Collin survived to when the gate opened, he would be tortured by Lucifer himself. This thought made James quite happy, and he hoped that it would come true. Knowing his luck, however, it wouldn't.

Bullets came raining down on the ground in front of James and hit Collin in the legs. Collin leaped back. James glanced over and found Seth was back up. He didn't appear completely healed, but it was enough.

Seth kept shooting, as he had an AR, which James still wasn't sure where he got it from. Those suckers held a lot more rounds than typical handguns. He wasn't sure why any human really needed one and found guns to be quite uncivilized. He preferred to fight with a sword or fists any day. It showed real skill.

While Collin was distracted, Gwen was able to stab Collin in the back with her sword. Collin let out a scream as he jumped forward out of the blade and turned and swung at her. Gwen clashed his blade with her own and started advancing on him.

Collin was beginning to slow down, James noted. Perhaps whatever was helping him had an expiration, or perhaps all those wounds were finally catching up to him. James watched as his energy started to diminish.

The light coming off him, however, didn't seem to falter.

So perhaps he wasn't weak. Perhaps he was faking it.

James decided to stay on the cautious side and act as if he were at full power. He couldn't afford to mess up. Glancing back, he found Jürgen was still healing but was getting there. The three of them could distract Collin while Jürgen opened up the gate.

Collin kept appearing weaker, but something seemed off about it. Although his senses were masked by all the energy coming from the gate, he didn't notice anything different about Collin. He still seemed the same. But if he were faking it, he was doing a good job as both Gwen and Seth slashed up his skin.

Then there was a flicker on Collin's lips.

Gwen noticed it before Seth and jumped back quickly. Seth, however, was not fast enough.

Collin's hand went right through Seth's chest, and in his hand he held his heart. In an instant, Seth vanished into dust.

"No!" Jürgen's voice came from behind them. James turned to find Jürgen pulling out his sword. "You two were supposed to deal with this hybrid!"

James wanted to say they were working on it, and the

two of them were supposed to get the gate open by now, but he figured it was not the time to piss off Jürgen. He jumped into action against Collin along with Jürgen and Gwen.

Collin realized Jürgen was not the person to make mad quickly.

Jürgen slashed and stabbed and pierced Collin. Gwen backed away as Jürgen wasn't caring what he hit as long as part of the time it was Collin. James had Jürgen's back, making sure the hybrid couldn't escape.

Collin went back and forth, trying to block what attacks he could as they both simultaneously attacked him. James had no idea what Gwen was doing, but suddenly smelled her blood. He turned his attention on her and found she was biting her own wrist.

What the hell?

She then got up close to Collin as if trying to force him to fly up. He did just that and grabbed her in the process.

What in the world was she thinking?

Gwen kissed Collin right on the lips.

Now James was just getting pissed, until he realized what she was doing. She was forcing him to drink her blood. She couldn't drink his, but what would happen if

Collin drank hers?

Except the problem was, Gwen was close enough to Collin where she could have taken out his heart right then and there, but she didn't. She wanted him to go back to being a hybrid. She wanted him for herself again.

James knew that Gwen loved him, but there was a small sliver somewhere in her heart for Collin as well. There was no way he would have all her love. Part of him broke at that moment.

Collin let out a scream. Whatever was causing him to glow and fly turned off like a light switch. He started to fall straight to the ground. And what he shouldn't have seen was that Gwen had grabbed Collin and put herself between the ground and him.

After all this, she still protected him from getting hurt.

She shoved him off herself and took a few deep breaths. Her bones were jetting out of her skin in some spots, and she started to heal herself. She grinned to them. "Well, that hurt."

James saw the fury on Jürgen's face and knew that he was not up to anything good. James ran as Jürgen went straight for Gwen.

CHAPTER THIRTY-FOUR

Gwen did not understand the series of events that happened before her.

Her mind backed up to why she was in the position she was in. It had occurred to her after she bit Collin that if she gave Collin her blood, whatever was possessing him would leave due to her demonic blood. So after Seth was killed and Jürgen went berserk, she took the opportunity to fill her mouth with her own blood. If Collin were back to his normal hybrid power, he would be easy to take out, or she could keep him around and let Lucifer handle him after they opened the doors to hell.

The only way she could do it, however, was if he grabbed her and flew her up in the sky. It was easy enough to get him to do that, as just like Gargoyles, anytime he was in close quarters with something that flew, they would take her up in the air with them. And just as she assumed, Collin did that.

So she kissed him and filled his mouth with her blood. What she didn't think about was how they were in the air and that she would go crashing down.

It hurt. It hurt bad. And as if just a reflex, she had put her body between Collin and the ground. She wasn't quite sure why she did that as she didn't think she still had feelings for Collin. Apparently her subconscious begged to differ. She wasn't sure how to process that and realized when she stood up she didn't have time to process any of it.

Because Jürgen was coming straight for her as if he was going to kill her.

Gwen didn't have time to react as she was still weak. The energy from the gate was coming into her, but not fast enough. Bones were broken and jutting out of her skin. It took everything she had to stand up. But before he got to her, the impossible happened.

James had jumped in front of Jürgen's hand.

Jürgen's hand was now straight into James's back. Gwen stared at James's face, horrified as to what may happen next. James's face was full of rage, pain, but still peered at her softly.

"You aren't going to let me kill Gwen, are you? Even after what she just did and what she could have done," Jürgen growled.

James made a little smile. "I will never let you kill her. She is my everything."

Gwen shook her head, tears falling down her cheeks. "No, don't. Please! I'm not worth this!"

"So be it!" Jürgen yelled as he did the one thing Gwen never thought possible—the one thing she never wanted to happen no matter what.

He pulled James's heart out of his chest, and James's being scattered into dust. Before he completely disappeared, Gwen watched as he mouthed his last words—*I love you.*

Gwen screamed as fury filled her being. Energy straight from the gate filled her with rage, anger, resentment—all of it gave her power. It was more power than she had ever possessed in her entire life.

"I am going to kill you!" Gwen yelled as she grabbed the sword James once had and began slashing viciously.

"Now you know how it feels, Gwen! Now you know the misery I felt when you destroyed the love of my life!" Jürgen exclaimed back as he countered each of her attacks.

Gwen didn't care that he had once loved a human that he was going to turn into a hybrid—that love was meaningless compared to hers and James's. They had fallen from Heaven for each other—they had sacrificed everything to be with each other. And now he was gone. Now he was in hell, experiencing eternal torture because of Jürgen.

She was going to kill Jürgen if it was the last thing she did.

When the doors to hell opened, it was said that the fallen Twelve would be able to walk the Earth once again. However, the moment James died, something inside her realized that wasn't true. The blood pact they had revealed the truth—they were never going to see this world again, even after everything.

So if the doors opened, would she be able to see James? Would she be able to die and go to hell to retrieve him and be with him? Or were those all lies?

When the door opened, would they all be thrown into hell while Lucifer ruled? Did it matter? If she couldn't be with James, then all this was for nothing.

All the bloodshed, all the humans and Gargoyles she had killed, were for nothing. James was dead—their bond told her that for sure. His body was gone, and he could never return. And it was all because of Jürgen.

She didn't hold back. Fury was driving her, and the more she gave in to those emotions, the more energy she felt come from the gate. She found it to be ironic since it was the gate she was never going to open as she wanted all this to be over once and for all.

And the only way to do that was to take down Jürgen.

This wasn't the first time they got into a heated battle, but this was the first time the two of them were going all out. Gwen had battled many Gargoyles, but never did she feel she fought like this. No, she was never as angry as this.

"You killed him! He will never be back!" She screamed as she tried to stab him again and again, but he countered all her moves.

"Why are you blaming me? If you had killed Collin while you were in the air instead of giving him your blood, I wouldn't have had to try to kill you! This is your fault!"

Gwen knew deep down he was right. She should have simply taken Collin's heart out at that moment. But something inside her never even thought about doing that.

Did she betray James with Collin? She didn't want to believe she did, as her love for James was bottomless, but she couldn't help having a soft spot for Collin. She wanted him to be happy because, for a short timeframe of her own existence, she had understood what it felt like to be human. And she had taken that humanity away from Collin. She hated that that happened to him and deep down kept wanting to make it up to him.

But that didn't change the fact they had been lied to —that Lucifer had said all the demons that fell to hell would be resurrected when the time came. That had been a lie. Lucifer always lied.

So she was going to do what she could to stop the gate from being opened. If she didn't get to have her wish, like hell was she going to let Lucifer get his.

First thing was first, however, and that was taking down Jürgen. He was the strongest physically out of all the Twelve, but hell hath no fury like a woman scorned. She had the will to defeat him. She needed to do it for

James.

Jürgen's attention drifted to Collin. "You know, before I kill you, I should kill your hybrid so you can watch both your loves die in the same day. Then you will know what it was like for me to find you standing over my dear Elizabeth Báthory's body."

"She was a psychotic human! You didn't have love! She was just using you for the power you promised!"

"No! She loved me for who I was! She loved me for being a demon, and I'll never find someone like her again! Unlike you, I won't be able to see the love of my life again!"

Gwen shook my head. "Lucifer's promises were lies! The Twelve that have fallen will never rise again! I can feel it!"

"Lucifer wouldn't lie to us! You are just upset because you watched James die!"

There was no use in talking to him. He was brainwashed like all the others had been—like she had been. But it was always one lie after another with him, and Gwen wasn't going to have any more of it. She was going to end Jürgen, and she was going to set everything right again. She had to—it was the only way.

And she was going to let Collin live the rest of his life before she took her own. He could finally get what he wanted and have a normal life.

Gwen slashed again and again at Jürgen, but he countered every attack. She wasn't getting tired—at least not yet—but she would have to rethink her battle strategy if she really wanted to take him down. She needed help.

She needed Collin to wake up and help her.

But would he? The last thing he would remember when he woke up would be her taking away hisAngelic powers. And that she was trying to kill him along with all the others. She just prayed that he would understand what happened and would side with her. He could kill her if he wanted, but that would more than likely kill him as well.

Gwen glanced over at him. He was still knocked out. *Come on*, she thought. *Wake up*!

CHAPTER THIRTY-FIVE

Collin dreamed the strangest dream.

He dreamed that he was standing on a cliff, and below him was a fire, and behind him was a bunch of people. He felt as if he had to get ready for the fire—as if he were the only thing stopping the entire world from getting burned. The flames were reaching higher and higher until finally they reached the top of the cliff. Collin didn't know what to do—there was no way he could ever stop all this fire.

As he thought the end was here and that he was going

to be burned alive, suddenly darkness filled the sky and rain came pouring down. He peered up and found that the clouds were taking over the fire. The flames grew smaller and smaller, and finally the risk was no more. Collin realized that it was the Heavens that had saved him. He needed to stop thinking that he was the only one in this fight. There was much more going on.

Collin looked down at the smoldering flames and saw a figure trying to stamp them out but who was on fire as well. She seemed to be frantically trying to stop it all by herself but wasn't doing a good job at it and was being swallowed up whole as well.

"Gwen?" he whispered.

Before he could do anything about the situation he was witnessing, he felt as if he were being pulled into another world. His eyes flickered open to find that he was back in Jerusalem, outside the tomb of Jesus.

What had happened, he wondered? The last thing he remembered was Gwen kissing him. Then he remembered tasting her blood and everything began to hurt.

She had forced her blood into him and tainted him, so whatever was helping him was gone.

Collin realized that was wrong, and that was what the

dream had been about. Heaven was still on his side, helping him out. He just had to have faith.

But then what was the part about Gwen? He tried to focus on what was going on around him even though his ears were still ringing. From that height, he should have been in a lot worse shape, but that wasn't the case. He would try to figure that out later—right now he had to figure out why Jürgen and Gwen were fighting.

Then he noticed it—James was nowhere to be seen.

What had happened to James? With the way that Gwen was acting, had Jürgen done something to him? But why would Jürgen hurt James? It made no sense. Unless Jürgen was going after Gwen for what she did to him, and James tried to stop him and that ended his life.

Collin had a feeling he had hit the nail on the head.

He wanted to help Gwen, mainly because it would be one more demon down and all he would have to do is destroy Gwen, but he was weak and had no way to heal himself. He needed blood again, just like before Erik had offered his own energy to Collin. Then Collin ruined the power he had by letting Gwen get close. He should have realized what she was doing, but he had been surrounded and didn't have anywhere else to go but up.

Collin realized Gwen could have killed him at that moment, and that was why the Gargoyles were always careful when they took the demons up in the air like they did. Demons in close quarters could cause a lot of problems, especially since they could bite or force blood down one's throat, or even take out one's heart. He was lucky that Gwen didn't do that.

But that was why Jürgen was so pissed at her.

Or at least that was what he figured. Gwen had risked everything to keep Collin alive and was now trying to take down her fellow demon comrade.

And Collin had to help her.

He needed to help her for a few reasons. First, because if she died, then he died and they couldn't stop Jürgen. Secondly, she had saved him, which led Collin to believe that perhaps she no longer wanted to open the gates to hell. He could be wrong, as Gwen seemed a bit fickle for what she wanted. Perhaps she wasn't, however, but she was just always fighting with her conscience. And it seemed the conscience had finally won.

The problem was, Collin still couldn't move. A thought occurred to him. If the demons could use the power coming from the gate as if it were blood, could he? He didn't like the idea of using a demonic force, but he had no other choice. He closed his eyes and focused.

He didn't hear the voice like he had last time, which Collin was thankful for. With how weak he was, he didn't know if he would have given in to what that voice was saying this time. He hoped he wouldn't, but he was in a lot of pain and just wanted to help Gwen. He felt the energy coming to him in the same way blood did—filling up his energy and being.

Opening his eyes, he found that he was at full force once again. It wasn't like how he was when he was using the power of the Archangel, but it was enough where he felt he could help Gwen.

He grabbed the sword that Gwen had dropped when he lifted her up in the sky. Although he didn't have as much experience with a sword as the demons did, he did spend years training with Hugo and prayed that he would be able to stand a chance. Between him and Gwen, he felt that he could do it.

Now the fight really did feel like the lightsaber battle in *The Phantom Menace*. He just prayed that neither Gwen nor he would be killed in this.

He swung at Jürgen while Jürgen was facing Gwen,

but Jürgen ducked, making Collin swing at nothing. Collin almost lost his stance, which would have been embarrassing as the first attack against his foe. Collin centered himself again and countered Jürgen's swing as Gwen swept her leg under Jürgen. Jürgen jumped up and swung toward Gwen.

This was Collin's chance.

Collin stabbed the sword in Jürgen's back where his heart should be. He could tell by the demon's yelp that he had been close, but not close enough. Jürgen elbowed Collin in the stomach, sending him flying back. Luckily Collin didn't lose his grip on the sword, and it slid out of Jürgen.

Jürgen was not someone to mess with. Collin already knew this, but it was hitting him moreso now that he had to fight him again.

But this was the end times—he couldn't run away. He had to help Gwen get her revenge and then deal with her after everything.

Gwen was sweating—her hair matted to her face, but she didn't seem to be letting up against Jürgen. Collin got back up and ran to help once again. They both swung at Jürgen, but Jürgen jumped out of the way, and Collin and Gwen clashed swords.

"Good to see you are fine now. You ready to end this?" Gwen asked as she turned her attention to Jürgen.

Collin nodded. "As ready as I'm ever going to be."

CHAPTER THIRTY-SIX

Gwen was surprised that Collin was back up again. After that fall, even though she had shouldered much of the force, she figured he wouldn't be standing for quite some time. She wondered if he was able to take energy from the gate now that he was back to being a hybrid and tied to her blood.

Either way, he was helping her fight, and that was all she needed.

Jürgen was a pain to fight—he was strong and skilled and had spent most of his spare time training. She had spent a lot time training, but really, she had goofed off with James.

"See Jürgen, if I didn't kill that lover of yours, you would have never grown to be this strong. I was doing you a favor."

Jürgen glared at her. "Perhaps if James weren't around, you would have been equally as strong."

"Oh, I know I would be. But I bet I'm a better lover than you."

Jürgen swung down hard at her, but she blocked it and stepped out of the way. Collin tried to attack Jürgen from behind again, but to no avail. She just wished one of them could get a good blow so she could get in close enough to either cut off his head or take out his heart.

Things could never be easy, could they?

Gwen took in a deep breath and focused. They both needed to attack at the same time to take Jürgen down. He was strong, and it was apparent he was used to taking on two opponents at the same time. Gwen wished he would show some kind of weakness, but so far he hadn't indicated any.

She was beginning to realize that she had messed up and she should have never pissed him off all those years ago.

Gwen knew it wasn't the fact that she had sabotaged their chance in opening the gate over seven decades before, nor was it the fact that she had helped Collin—all the anger that Jürgen was showing was due to the fact that she had killed Elizabeth Bathory—the only love he had ever had.

At the time, she really didn't think he loved her that much. She thought she was using him to get power and that they were just wasting time. They had made a treaty never to make a hybrid, and yet Jürgen was going to give her that power.

So what else was she supposed to do when she found out the truth about him? She had to do something or else that women was going to go berserk.

She hadn't been stable to begin with—who knew what trouble she was going to get in once she became a hybrid? Gwen knew the type of human she was—one who wanted power and wasn't going to listen to any orders given to her. She did what she wanted and thought herself a god, or something along those lines. That was probably why Jürgen liked her so much, but if she wasn't going to follow what they said to begin with, how were they going to keep her in check?

Gwen should have just let him turn her. She probably

would have taken out a plethora of Gargoyles and demons before they took her out. Then she would have had less work to do. But that was a long time ago, and he was still pissed at her.

She never realized how much he really did care about her.

But Jürgen would never realize how much stronger the bond between James and her was. Jürgen didn't understand the sacrifices they made to be together. He only loved Elizabeth Bathory for her beauty and lust for blood, but he didn't sacrifice his entire world for her—he didn't give up Heaven for her. No, Jürgen gave up Heaven for power—a power that would never be given to him.

And a love that would never be given to James and Gwen.

Gwen pushed back the tears that began to fill her eyes once again. She couldn't let anything obstruct her vision as she was fighting to save everything she cared about. All she had left now was Collin, and she was going to make her wish for him come true. Then, once it was fulfilled, she could die and find her place in hell for all eternity.

And at least she and James would be tortured

together.

She would finally pay for all the blood she had shed —all the acts of evil she had committed. Granted, the torture would be for disappointing Lucifer, but she had to look at it a different way. It was going to be the worst experience of all her life, and it would never end. If she was a normal person, she would do her best never to go to hell, but she considered herself a bit of a masochist. One had to be to deal with all the things around them.

No matter how many times she swung at Jürgen, he didn't flinch or miss blocking her or Collin. It didn't seem he was tiring, but at least neither was she. This battle could last hours, and they would still be going full force.

If only something would come and help her. If only they had more power.

But that wasn't going to happen. The three of them were the only ones left. There were no demons or Gargoyles left other than those who were standing there right then. Gwen missed the days when all twelve on each side were still alive and were going all out in fights. It was chaotic—the one thing she loved most about the world. She didn't like order as it was boring. She liked to mix it up, and that was exactly what she had been doing for the past four thousand years or so.

And that was why she was now paying the price.

Gwen wished she could have seen James one last time. She would miss his human form and how beautiful his body was. She would miss the way his skin felt on hers, the way his teeth sank into her neck, the way his blood tasted on her lips.

Yes, Gwen would take down Jürgen if it was the last thing she did.

If she could have her way, she would get to torture Jürgen for a while before sending him to the special place that Lucifer had waiting for all the Twelve who failed. But she knew she had to be quick or he could come back and destroy her. He always did heal quite quickly.

Then it occurred to her—she had pocketed something just in case she would need it.

Gwen pulled out the triduanum and swung it at Jürgen. He glared at her.

"Really Gwen? You brought that to a fight where the Gargoyles could have stolen it from you and killed you?"

"Well, it seems to me I brought it just in case I got stabbed in the back."

"Oh, I will be sure to stab you in the back with it."

Jürgen turned and kicked Collin, sending him straight back. Jürgen sheathed his sword in a quick movement and grabbed both her wrists.

"Shit," Gwen whispered as she fought with all her strength against Jürgen.

"Yeah, you didn't think this one through, now did you? I am and always have been stronger than you, Guinevere. But I think you need a little reminder."

Jürgen snapped her wrist back, and she let out a cry of pain. Now that her grip had been weakened, Jürgen grabbed the triduanum and stabbed in her chest, right next to her heart. Gwen fell to the ground, a black web spreading across her chest. She let out a scream.

"Now, while you are there withering in pain, you can watch as your precious hybrid dies."

Jürgen turned to go deal with Collin. Gwen's eyes were full of tears, both for the man she had lost, the man she would lose, and for the pain that was spreading throughout her body.

It was too much for her, and the world began to spin and everything went black.

CHAPTER THIRTY-SEVEN

Collin wasn't sure how he was going to survive.

Gwen was done, as she had brought that special knife that hurt demons, and Jürgen had quickly turned it on her. She had loss consciousness, and for some odd reason, Jürgen didn't finish her right then and there. Perhaps he wanted to kill Collin first and make her watch.

That seemed sadistic enough for him to do. Collin wouldn't put it past him.

There was no demon blood for Gwen to drink to heal

her besides Jürgen. She wasn't going to be healing anytime soon. Collin would have to defeat Jürgen on his own. He wasn't sure if that would even be possible, as Collin had never defeated a demon before except when he was being possessed, but that didn't count in his mind. And Jürgen was strong—stronger than the others. That much was for certain.

Jürgen came on him with his full strength, slashing and stabbing with his sword. Collin was able to hold back the demon, but with every passing moment, he felt as if the sword was going to be flung out of his hands.

He didn't know what he was going to do. There was no way he was going to defeat him.

Jürgen grinned. "What's the matter? Now that you don't have your girlfriend or that Archangel possessing you, are you completely helpless?"

Collin gritted his teeth. "No, it's just that I don't do well with one-to-one combat. I prefer a group on both sides. That way people can move back and forth and I don't feel so alone."

"Yeah, not because you rely on them. You should know by now in our line of work, you can't rely on anyone, not even your comrades."

For a moment, Jürgen seemed to be distracted by his

thoughts. Collin wondered if he could use that to his advantage. "Oh why? It seems like all you demons had the same goal in opening the gate to hell."

That was clearly not true as Jürgen hadn't been trying to open it since Collin killed Seth. Jürgen glared at him, but his movements were now slower.

"No, not all the demons have the same goals, clearly. Gwen hasn't wanted to open the gates for quite some time. She shouldn't have been trusted and should have been killed a long time ago for betraying us."

"But James wouldn't let that happen, now would he?" Collin found that this was working—he no longer felt as if he were going to lose his life in an instant. Now he felt he had at least five minutes, tops.

"No, he wouldn't. He gave up everything for her, and she just tossed him aside in her search for redemption. There is no redemption for us, and she knows it. She should have just kept working at our original goal so that she and James could be together forever. But instead, she risked it all for you."

It didn't seem that way to Collin. In his eyes, Gwen loved James more than anything. Collin was just like a cute puppy rather than someone she truly wanted to be with. But he supposed it didn't seem that way to the rest of them. "I don't know. It seemed she was willing to give up everything for him. But then you ruined that when you killed him—or, at least, I presume that was what happened. I was kind of passed out."

"And she could have taken that time to kill you, but she didn't. She betrayed him and didn't deserve love. She hasn't deserved love for quite some time."

Even with all this talking, Jürgen was blocking all Collin's strikes. He wished the demon would slow down, but it was apparent that wasn't going to happen.

"And because she killed the woman you loved?" Collin asked and immediately realized it was a mistake.

A punch came straight toward his stomach and sent him flying backward. Collin hit the ground with a loud thud.

"She killed her for no reason! Gwen is a bitch and deserves to be tortured for eternity for the shit she pulls each and every day. She doesn't care about anyone except herself, and yet she just keeps getting away with it. Well, not anymore. I am through."

Jürgen grabbed his sword and started stabbing it at Collin as he was still on the ground. Collin rolled each and every way, avoiding the blade.

This demon was scary when he was pissed. He

wished he had taken him out before he took out Seth.

"And then what happens?" Collin asked, almost out of breath. "Do you get a crown or something for being the demon that opens the gate? Do you get all your wishes to come true?"

"No! Because my wish to be with her will never be granted! She is dead, and nothing can bring back the dead."

"But that isn't why you fell from Heaven. What was the original wish you had?"

Jürgen hesitated, as if he didn't remember anymore. Had it been power? Collin wondered. Had it been freedom?

Jürgen paused long enough where Collin could sweep his leg underneath him, and Jürgen fell backward. Collin took the time to stand back and was about to hurry to try to stab Jürgen, but he was back on his feet already.

Damn how fast he was.

"You aren't going to be able to take me out. I have everything to win by killing you and everything to lose if I die. If you die, you just go to Heaven, and they will tell you how you were a good boy and tried your best. If I die, I will be tortured for an eternity."

It was nice to hear from a demon that he would be going to Heaven and not hell. He had been a bit worried after what the voice had told him earlier. "Not my fault you picked the wrong side. But I ain't going to let you take me out. I am not letting my home be destroyed by Lucifer and all the demons in the underworld."

Jürgen raised his sword. "Well then, so be it."

CHAPTER THIRTY-EIGHT

White light was surrounding Gwen. She blinked her eyes open and found she was no longer in front of the tomb and gate to hell, but in a place that had no physical form.

"What the heck?" she whispered as she peered around. What was this place? Why was she here? Was this hell? It was a lot brighter than she imagined it to be.

Wait, she thought. I know this place. She narrowed her eyes. There was no way she could be back here, not after what she had done.

"Your thoughts are correct—you are technically not allowed back to Heaven."

She turned to find Erik standing there. She let out a laugh.

"Reading my mind now? I wouldn't advise that. It's pretty wicked up in there."

"Sarcastic until the very end. I didn't used to like that about you. You know that?" Erik said as he stepped forward. He was wearing an all white robe. She expected a halo, but none was there. That would have been overkill.

"Why am I here? Did I get to come see what I was missing before you all send me to hell?"

Erik took a deep, slow breath. "You are on the brink of dying, yes, but that's not exactly what is going on here."

She furrowed her brows at him. "What, is this like some kind of redeeming time for me like in a movie? I know I can't ever return here. I have accepted that."

"I know, Gwen. But you still want to stop the gates from being open, right?" Erik raised an eyebrow.

She slowly nodded. "I do. I realized… I realized everything Lucifer said was a lie. I mean, I have always known, but when James died… I felt it—I felt that he would never be let on Earth again, and if he can't come back, there was no way I was going to let Lucifer get his way."

"That is a selfish reason to want to save the world, but we will take it." Erik stepped forward. "Drink my blood one last time, and you will be healed from the triduanum. Then you can lock the gate with this." Erik held up an orb-looking thing. "And it will never be able to be opened again."

She raised an eyebrow. "Are you serious? Can I even drink your blood? Isn't this just some kind of ridiculous dream?"

He shrugged. "Perhaps. But only one way to find out."

Gwen let out a chuckle. "You Gargoyles never did play fair. But all right—I will close the gate. Just promise me that Collin will get to live out his life, and I will be able to die and be with James."

Erik nodded. "All right. But do realize while being with James, you two will be tortured forever."

"Yeah, I know. But better tortured together than apart. Besides, we are pretty into S and M."

Erik shook his head in disgust. "Just drink my blood,

and go close the gate."

Gwen stepped forward and bit into Erik's blood. It felt like it was the real deal as the warm, sweet blood filled her being. Perhaps this wasn't a dream. Perhaps she really was in Heaven, or at least the very outskirts of it.

Suddenly her eyes shot open. Gwen peered down to find that the effects of the triduanum were gone. She no longer had black poison lines stretching out across her body. No, she felt great, and she felt as if she could do anything.

The triduanum was still sticking out of her. She pulled it out, and her wound quickly healed. *Take that, Jürgen.* She examined her surroundings and hoped that Collin was still holding his own while she was out. Gwen found that Jürgen and Collin were still fighting by sword. She let out the breath that she had been holding.

He was still alive. She could do this.

She stood up and didn't let another moment waste as she ran over and stabbed Jürgen straight in the back with the triduanum. He let out a cry of pain.

"Take that, you asshole!" She yelled as she pulled the knife out and stabbed him again. "This is for trying to kill me!" Gwen exclaimed and stabbed again. "This is for killing James!" She threw the triduanum to the ground and jabbed her hand straight into his heart. "And this is for taking away my happiness."

She pulled out his heart, and Jürgen disappeared in front of her. Gwen took a couple of deep breaths and turned to Collin.

"Thank goodness for those cheaters in Heaven. Am I right?"

Collin stared at her, perplexed. "How are you fine?"

She held out a finger. "Hold that thought. I gotta go fix the gate."

He stood up as if he were going to stop her. She shook her head.

"Don't worry, I won't open it. Erik gave me something to seal it once and for all."

Collin narrowed his eyes. "How do I know you are telling the truth?"

She shrugged. "You don't, to be honest. I have never been one to tell the truth ever. You will just need to have faith."

Collin took a slow breath, but he didn't come closer. She turned back to the gate. She could feel the energy screaming against it, as if it were slamming its fists, wanting out. Lucifer was going to be pissed over what she was about to do.

Gwen focused on the light that Erik had given her, and suddenly it was in front of her again. She grabbed it, the Heavenly energy burning her hands as she threw it straight into the gate.

The force of Heavenly light exploded off the gate and threw Gwen back at great force. She smacked into the side of a rock, and suddenly everything went dark.

CHAPTER THIRTY-NINE

Collin knew Gwen wasn't dead since he was standing there.

But the dark energy that had been pouring out of the area was gone. She had really done it—she had shut the gate down for good.

He ran over to where her body lay. It looked as if it really, really hurt. She would need blood, and since he felt he was still strong, he could offer his.

Was that all right, though? Shouldn't he kill her? Shouldn't he end the one demon on Earth? He stood above her, not sure what he should do. She was the last evil that still existed—without her, all the rest of the minions would be dead. Then he would finally be free.

He collapsed next to her, sobbing. He couldn't do it. She had risked everything for him—he was the reason her lover was dead and why she betrayed her kind. Or at least he was part of the reason.

Collin couldn't bring himself to kill her. No, he needed her. They could live out the rest of their days fixing what the demons had messed up, and then when the time finally came, they could die and never see each other ever again. Gwen could go to James, and Collin could see his Gargoyles friends once again.

He brought his wrist to his mouth and bit it, letting his mouth fill with blood.

CHAPTER FORTY

Instead of complete light, Gwen found herself surrounded in darkness. This was it—she was in hell, and she would be here for the rest of eternity. She closed her eyes and let out a deep breath. She had done it—she had redeemed herself in her own eyes, and that was all that mattered.

"Open your eyes, sleepyhead. You aren't dead yet."

Her eyes opened, and she found that James was standing in front of her. She jumped into his arms and began crying.

"I'm sorry! It's all my fault! I didn't want it to end like this, I swear! I wanted to be together forever."

"But we were lied to. I understand now. I'm sorry I didn't listen to or believe your doubts."

She let him hold her for as long as she could, even as she felt a tug to try to wake up. She wished she would just die so she could stay in this darkness. James, however, was the one who backed away.

"I just came to tell you that you were right—we would have never gotten eternity forever. Go and fix the world. I will be waiting for you here."

She leaned in and kissed him. "I love you. I will always love you."

"I know. I have always known you have loved me. Just promise me to be happy, okay? It will keep me going until you are back."

She nodded, and suddenly everything disappeared and she felt lips upon hers. Gwen's eyes flickered open, and she found Collin feeding her his blood. It was nowhere as filling or sweet as James's, but it would have to do.

Collin noticed that she was awake and backed off. She glanced around. She really did do it—she had closed the gate once and for all. She peered back to Collin and raised an eyebrow.

"Why didn't you kill me when you had the chance?"

He shrugged. "Figured at this point there was no need. And because you needed to fix what you messed up."

She laughed. "Yeah, I suppose I do. Then you can go back to your life in London."

He slowly nodded. "Yeah, we could, couldn't we?"

Gwen's eyes widened. She didn't think he would want her back—accept her in his boring life. She shrugged. "Maybe for a bit. I don't age, so I think people might notice."

"Oh right. I probably won't either, will I?"

She shook her head. "No, sorry."

He held out his hand. "I guess we will have to keep traveling the world, won't we?"

She took his hand and stood up. "I guess we will. Until Lucifer makes his centurial visit to Earth and drags me to hell himself."

"So we have 100 years?"

"Yup."

"Well then, where should we start?"

She glanced around. The world seemed brighter and more peaceful already. "I think we should start with finding the nearest road. Hopefully a car can pick us up and take us to a city or something."

He laughed. "That sounds like a plan to me."

Thank you so much for reading! Readers like you make it possible for authors like me to write stories! If you could spare a moment and leave a review on Amazon, Goodreads, BookBub, and wherever you like to buy books, that would mean the world to me! It really helps authors like me to succeed in the publishing world.

Acknowledgements

This novel has been many years in the making and am so excited to finally get it out for readers to enjoy. There are many people who helped make this possible, including my mentors Mike, Joe, Betty, Paul, and many more over the years. I also want to give a big thank you to my editors Chantelle and Justin who have been encouraging me to keep writing since we first met, and to my new editor and friend Hilary who found interest in my story and wanted to be involved. I also want to say thank you to my writing group, Bernie, Traci, Rebecca, Stacy, and Christi who have been so helpful and great readers, editors, and listeners. To my friends, including Earlene, Veronica, Faye, Dave, and Amelia who helped edit and give feedback, thank you as well! Thank you Biserka Designs for the wonderful cover! To my parents who have helped through the years to keep on going. And lastly, to my husband who has stuck by my side, helping me through it all.

About the Author

Dani Hoots is a science fiction, fantasy, romance, and young adult author who loves anything with a story. She has a B.S. in Anthropology, a Masters of Urban and Environmental Planning, a Certificate in Novel Writing from Arizona State University, and a BS in Herbal Science from Bastyr University.

Currently she is working on a YA urban fantasy series called Daughter of Hades, a YA urban fantasy series called The Wonderland Chronicles, a historic fantasy vampire series called A World of Vampires, and a YA sci-fi series called Sanshlian Series. She has also started up an indie publishing company called FoxTales

Press. She also works with Anthill Studios in creating comics through Antik Comics.
Her hobbies include reading, watching anime, cooking, studying different languages, wire walking, hula hoop, and working with plants. She is also an herbalist and sells her concoctions on FoxCraft Apothecary. She lives in Phoenix with her husband and visits Seattle often. Feel free to email her with any questions you might have!
danihootsauthor@gmail.com

www.ingramcontent.com/pod-product-compliance
Lightning Source LLC
Chambersburg PA
CBHW070917260626
47162CB00007B/2706